WHEN NIGHTMARES FALL

EDITED BY ELIZABETH HARVEY

DIVERTIR
PUBLISHING
Salem, NH

When Nightmares Fall
Edited by Elizabeth Harvey

All stories contained in this manuscript
Copyright © 2010 by the respective authors

Cover photo by Elizabeth Harvey
Cover design by Elizabeth Harvey and Kenneth Tupper

Published by Divertir Publishing LLC
PO Box 232
North Salem, NH 03073
http://www.divertirpublishing.com/

ISBN-13: 978-0-9842930-0-1
ISBN-10: 0-9842930-0-0

Printed in the United States of America

To JP, without whom I would never get anything done, and to KT for giving me the chance to do what I dream.

— Elizabeth Harvey

Contents

Preface

As the premiere book for Divertir Publishing, this collection is the culmination of a significant effort by everyone involved. It has been an experience that will not soon be forgotten. The learning curve was steep but incredibly rewarding, and it is with great pride and pleasure that I write this introduction. The writers in this collection are nothing short of wonderful, both as people and as authors. I'm very excited to share these authors and their stories with you. I believe they are truly skilled in their craft, and I thank them for sharing their writing with us.

These stories came together after I decided to create a collection that would appeal to readers while capitalizing on what people I knew were writing. The "supernatural suspense" genre kept coming up again and again. It's one of my favorite genres and one that I find most satisfying as a writer. It is also what most of the authors I know tend to focus on — birds of a feather, after all. My goal was to showcase the skill of these authors and help them achieve their aspirations.

Having the ability to help people achieve their dreams is a heady wine that I hope you will share with me as we salute and celebrate the beginning of what we know will be an exciting step in the writing careers of these fantastic individuals.

— *Elizabeth Harvey*

The House That

Jack Built

by Verena Sandford

I'm glad it's not one of those dark, stormy nights, Jack thought to himself as he entered the house and imagined what it would look like illuminated by lightning. It was creepy enough anyway. The estate agent unsuccessfully clicked the light switch up and down several times before he sighed. "Sorry about this. They must have cut off the electricity."

"Doesn't matter," Jack said and held up his torch, "I'm prepared." He stepped into the large hall and looked around. Despite the darkness, he could get an idea of what this house was all about. It was old, with a musty, vacant smell about it, and Jack had a vague idea that it already had that smell when it was last occupied. Taking a deep breath, he imagined the previous owners as being nearly as old as the house: an elderly couple with white hair, each hunched over leaning on their walking sticks. Jack turned on the torch and shone it around the hall. *The high ceilings are nice*, he thought before walking into the sitting room.

The size of the room struck him. It was large enough to throw a gala in, and the parquet flooring certainly looked very inviting. Through the large bay window he could see the front garden, which consisted solely of tall trees and bushes nearly blocking out the light. The far wall was almost entirely taken up by the largest marble fireplace Jack had ever seen. The ceiling was high, like in the hall, and had a magnificent ceiling rose in the middle. Jack could just see a crystal chandelier hanging from it. He adored the room.

He moved on to the dining room, which was large enough to host a dinner party for ten. Jack smiled at the thought of Helen cooking dinner for ten guests, as she was not the best cook in the world and certainly not very keen on it. If it were up to her, they would probably get a take out for ten. He saw the back garden through the bay window and walked over to have a look outside. Although he couldn't see much, by now he wasn't sure if he cared what the garden looked like. Just the ground floor was so full of potential, and he loved it.

He tried to calm himself down and look at it realistically — it was old, needed a lot of work, and would probably be very expensive to fix. To test this theory, he pushed his car key into the window frame only to be disappointed with the ease with which it went in. The fact that all the windows had to be treated for dry rot only reinforced his pessimism. Looking down, he saw that the floorboards were peppered with holes created by long-dead woodworms. Crouching, he took a screwdriver out of his coat pocket, shoved it between two of the boards, and used it to lever one of them up. It came up with unfortunate ease, allowing Jack to see the ground. Pulling out his torch, he flicked it on and shone the light into the dark hole. Rat droppings covered the ground and Jack winced. If there was one thing he couldn't stand, it was rats. He turned the beam and the light fell on a little tray full of blue pellets. Rat poison. At least that was good news; the droppings were probably old. He lowered the board and shoved the screwdriver back into his pocket before he rubbed his hands together, blowing on them. Damn place was freezing.

The estate agent looked out the window. Jack found him unusually quiet for an estate agent and suspected that even he could not find anything good to say about the place. He replaced the floorboard. "How long has this house been vacant?" he asked.

The agent turned around and smiled at Jack. "About three months." The dust around the place suggested otherwise, and Jack was sure that he was lying. He decided not to go into it. "It has come back onto the market quite unexpectedly," the man continued. "The previous owner bought it as an investment but had problems with his finances and had to pull out. Quite sad, actually. He was very distressed."

Jack was barely listening. He checked out the kitchen and

breakfast room and could not see anything that did not need a lot of work done to it. The conservatory looked quite new, but during the recent storms a branch from one of the trees had fallen onto the glass roof and shattered it into thousands of pieces. Nobody had bothered to do anything about it, and the subsequent rain had spoiled the wooden flooring.

He started to go upstairs. "Mind the second step." He heard the estate agent's warning just in time. Instead of stepping over it, he lifted the carpet and looked at the step. It sported a hole about the size of a foot. Jack left the carpet up and stepped over it.

The house was enormous. The six bedrooms were good sizes and each one had a fireplace, though the ceilings in two of the rooms looked close to collapse. One of the fireplaces had fallen over, and the marble was cracked in various places. Still Jack loved it and was trying hard to contain his enthusiasm. "It hasn't got central heating, then?" he asked the agent, even though he already knew the answer. He brushed a cobweb that was almost black with dust out of his way while he listened to the other man's awkward excuses. Thinking about the house's potential, he went to a window and gazed outside.

From up here the view was magnificent. The house was at the end of the village, overlooking it like a castle on the top of a little hill. Behind it were only fields and woodlands. Jack stood and looked, and wondered how he could sell this idea to his wife. Eventually he turned around.

"I'll think about it," Jack said noncommittally. The agent

nodded, though he didn't expect Jack to buy it. Truthfully, he couldn't imagine anybody wanting to buy this old ruin. They shook hands and parted company. Jack was so excited he could barely stop himself from running to his car. He forced himself to walk slowly and made sure he did not look around as he walked. If he wanted to get the price down he could not give the impression that he was really bothered about buying this place.

§ § §

"Honey, I swear to you, the place is perfect," Jack said for the fifth time. Helen was still unconvinced. "I can do it up myself. It's a lot of work, but I'm a builder and I have a lot of friends in the trade who can help me out cheaply. It's going well under price, and I might get some more off if I try. Please, honey, think about it! You don't have to live there. It's just an investment, but it will pay off big time!"

"I don't know, Jack," Helen said, but he heard in her voice she was beginning to come round. "It will be so much work, and I know you. You will spend every spare minute up there and I'll hardly ever get to see you. And what happens if you can't sell it when it's done? After all, it's in some tin pot village in the middle of nowhere—who wants to live there?"

Well, I for one wouldn't mind getting out of London, Jack thought. "People will kill to get that house when I'm finished with it." Helen smiled, and Jack took that as a good sign. He put his arms around her and kissed her. "Please?" he said. She sighed and nodded and Jack felt a wave of relief. That had gone better than expected.

The next day he phoned the estate agent, deliberately putting on a rather bored voice and offering £50,000 less than the asking price. He knew that was a bit bold of him, but figured if the offer was rejected he could always up the bid. A couple of hours later the estate agent rang back. The offer had been accepted. Jack was speechless. The house had been cheap to begin with, but now it was almost a gift. He had never heard of a silly offer like this one being accepted first time, and a small, niggling doubt came into his mind. Maybe the house was worse than he thought. He had only seen it in the dark and never paid attention to the roof. What if it had subsidence? He bit his lip, worried that his decision had been rushed, but then brushed his doubts aside. It was too cheap to expect anything more than a ruin. He had always been proud to say that he was a good builder, so here was his chance to prove it.

§§§

Jack whistled as he climbed up onto the ladder. The gas and electricity had still not been reconnected, but Jack expected someone to do so later that morning. He shivered and considered lighting a fire in the big, marble fireplace, then decided against it. Better not light that old thing before a chimney sweep had given it the once-over. But this house sure was cold.

The first task was to get some light into the place. He gave the dark, heavy velvet curtains a tug and they came tumbling down, together with the curtain rail and part of the rendering. Jack fell backward off the ladder and landed on the wooden floor, winding himself in the process. Not a good start, he thought as he slowly clambered to his feet again. He swore and gave the curtains a good kick.

He worked late that night. Helen had been right, he thought, feeling guilty, but he could not tear himself away from the house. He had made a lot of progress in one day, and if he could just finish this…

"Jack."

He looked around. "Helen?" he asked, stunned that she had made the trip out to the house, especially at this time of day. It was nearly dark outside, and Helen didn't like driving in the dark. "I'm in the master bedroom, honey!" he called to her. When he did not hear her answer, he went to the window and looked outside. Her car was not in the drive. *What the hell did she do with the car*, he thought. "Helen? Where are you? Come upstairs, will you?"

Again, he heard no answer. He was getting annoyed now. Just a few more minutes and he would have finished for the day. He stormed down the stairs. The front door was closed and there was no sign of Helen. "Helen?" he shouted, now concerned. He could not find her anywhere. Just to be sure, he dialed her number on his mobile phone. She answered instantly. "Where are you?" he barked at her.

"What do you mean, where am I?" she asked, and Jack

could hear she was annoyed. "I'm in the kitchen throwing your dinner in the rubbish bin. Where the hell are you?"

Jack was confused. "You haven't been at the house?"

"No, I haven't, and you better not be there much longer if you want to live," she said, and hung up on him.

Slowly, Jack put the mobile down. He was sure he had heard her call his name. He grinned uneasily and rubbed his temples, feeling silly. It was probably just a floorboard creaking or something. He went back upstairs and finished what he was doing. On his way home he stopped at a garage and bought some flowers for Helen. It wasn't a good idea to get on the wrong side of her on the first day.

§ § §

"Jack."

He spun around, this time sure it wasn't Helen. She had made it quite clear that she would not drive all the way out to the house to see him. If he wanted to see her, he knew where she was. Someone was in the house—a squatter maybe. The house had been empty for a while, and it was possible that someone had moved in before him. "Hello?" he called. "Who's there?"

"Jack," he heard someone say.

He could not work out where the voice was coming from. It was a woman calling him, an older woman by the sound of it. "How do you know my name?" he called. He picked up a hammer and started walking from room to room. The woman did not answer him.

"Listen, lady, I own this house now, so you better find somewhere else to live, okay?"

He heard faint laughter. "Of course you own it, dear," he heard the woman say. The voice was coming from behind him and he turned around quickly, bracing himself. There was nobody there. He walked back into the room he had just checked, thinking she must have managed to sneak in when his back was turned, but the room was empty.

"And what is this nonsense about living somewhere else?" The voice came from the ground floor. How the hell had she got there that quickly? Jack ran down the stairs. "We live here together, dear, like we always have ever since you built this house."

The kitchen. Jack was paying little attention to what she was saying—she was obviously deranged—and when he found her he would turn her out and that would be the end of it. Nevertheless, he was cautious. He pushed the kitchen door open with his foot, holding the hammer in both hands, ready for her to attack him with whatever weapon she might have armed herself with.

The kitchen was empty. Jack blinked twice to make sure, but wasn't entirely surprised. The old crow knew her way around the house; she probably crept out the back door while he was tiptoeing up to the front. The back door was ajar and Jack relaxed a little, lowering the hammer. He crossed the kitchen quickly and bolted the door. There. That should keep her out. Just to make sure he called out. "Hello?" When she did not answer he felt silly. He went back upstairs and looked at the work he had been doing. He did not feel like finishing it that night and tossed the hammer down. The ceiling would have to wait until tomorrow.

§ § §

The first thing he spotted as he drove up to the house was the lights. Finally they had managed to turn the electricity back on. Jack mumbled a couple of swear words under his breath, thinking the lights had probably been on all day. He got out of the car and briefly noted that the lights were on in every room. What was the probability that the light switch had been left on in every room? He considered the thought, and came to the conclusion that it was probably the squatter again. Not only had she found a way back in, but she also turned all the lights on. Jack grimaced; he really did not need this aggravation.

He tried the door. It was locked. So this was not where she had got in. The back door was bolted from the inside—he had made sure before he went home the night before. He walked around the house and found all the windows closed. He tried them one by one. They were locked from the inside, and he cursed again. The old woman must have tricked him into thinking she left the house when really she had been in there all along.

He unlocked the door and went inside. The place was freezing, much colder than he would have expected. He slammed the door behind him. "All right, lady, listen up! I know that you are in here—you've left all the lights…" Jack walked into the sitting room and stopped in mid sentence. Someone had lit the fire. It was burning high and generating quite a bit of heat. There were candles on the mantelpiece. The room would have looked very cozy had it not been for the odd circumstances. Despite the heat from the fire, Jack was shivering. Damn, this house was cold!

The curtains were drawn. Jack was sure they had been open a minute ago when he walked around the house, so she must have just closed them. A sudden realization hit him as he stared at the curtains. Of course they had been open before. He had taken them down two days ago to let some light in through the windows, and he had not yet put them back. And not only the curtains, but the rails had come down as well. They had been replaced.

Jack felt faint. He walked over to the curtains and touched them almost shyly. They had been cleaned. More so, if he had not known better he would have sworn they were brand new. How had she done that? He dismissed the question. There was no way an old lady had cleaned the heavy velvet curtain, replaced the curtain rails and hung them back up all by herself. Somebody had helped her. There was somebody else living here, and even then this was nothing short of a miracle.

"Welcome home, Jack," she said behind him.

He turned quickly on his heels, and again he was faced with nothing but emptiness and questions begging to be answered. Had he thought before that she was old? He must have been mistaken. Her voice was young and seductive. "Where are you, lady?" This was getting ridiculous. "I'm not going to play games with you again. You come out now or I call the police!" Jack shouted, louder than he had intended to, and realized that he was a little bit afraid. He checked the room for a tool he could use, anything he could carry that would make him feel less vulnerable, but the room was empty. Spotless, actually. The parquet floor looked like it had been freshly waxed, and Jack groaned involuntarily. He didn't like feeling insecure, allowing his irrationality to manipulate his common sense. What the hell was going on? He had heard that squatters live in filth, but squatters that clean the house for you and repair curtain rails? There had to be another explanation.

He walked into the dining room and winced when he saw that the roof in the conservatory was no longer leaking. The glass had been replaced, as had the second step on the staircase. Jack walked up the stairs with his back to the wall. He scolded himself for being childish, but at the same time did not move away from the wall. He did not know how many there were and it was better to be safe than sorry.

When he got to the top of the stairs, he was not really surprised to see that the work he had not finished the previous night was now done. The ceilings had been stabilized, the fallen fireplace refitted, and the rooms decorated. His tools were neatly stacked in a corner. He picked up the hammer, and after a moment's consideration took a spanner for good measure. Despite the freezing cold, sweat was dripping off his forehead and running into his eyes. He wiped it away with his sleeve.

"What's going on here?" he whispered. His eyes were darting around the rooms as he moved quietly around the second floor. He did not see anybody.

"Welcome home, Jack," he heard the woman's voice.

He screamed. The voice came from the master bedroom. Jack had just been in there and it had been empty. Jack had the almost overwhelming urge to run.

"Come to me, Jack! It has been so long! Come to me, my darling!"

Jack stopped in his tracks. Her voice was so sexy, so… longing. Who was she? Why did she call him? Suddenly Jack had to find out what she looked like. He turned and walked to the master bedroom. "How do you know my name?" he asked as he opened the door.

The woman was lying on the bed, covered only by a satin sheet. Only there was no bed and no sheet. The illusion was wavering, like an old black and white picture projected onto a moving cloth. The woman smiled at Jack but she was not there, either. Jack could see the wall and the floor through her and shivered. This room was positively freezing.

"Why, you are my husband, dear," she said with a hint of impatience in her voice. She stretched her arms out to him. "You built this house for me, but then you left. I was alone for such a long time, but now you are back and everything will be all right. I feel so young, so good. Come to me, my darling. Make love to me now and we will be together forever."

When Jack took an involuntary step back, the look on her face changed. She sat up in the illusory bed, clutching the satin

13

sheet to cover herself up. "What is it, Jack? Why don't you want me?"

Jack was trembling. He raised his tools and noticed how much his hands were shaking. "Now, look, lady..." he began, but she did not let him finish his sentence. She floated out of the bed and toward Jack faster than he could back away. He tripped over his toolbox and landed hard on his back. She hovered above him.

"Lady?" she hissed. She raised her hands as if to grab him, and Jack frantically crawled backward to get away. "Why are you calling me that, Jack? I am your Claudine! I am your wife, and I demand that you treat me like that! Why won't you kiss me? Have you met another woman? Is that why you have been away so long?"

With every word she seemed to age, and Jack had time to realize that the house aged with her. Out of the corner of his eyes he could see the ceiling sagging, the fireplace falling and breaking, and when he reached the second step, coming tumbling down the stairs head first, he found that broken too. His hand went through the hole desperately seeking something to hold on to as he fell all the way down, and he screamed when a piece of wood pierced his arm. The woman was still following him, hovering over him. She now looked ancient, and when she opened her mouth again part of the skin covering her face ripped and allowed Jack insight into her head. He screamed and hysterically pulled on his arm to free it.

"What is it, Jack?" she asked. "Don't you love me anymore?" Jack ripped his arm out of the broken wood, not caring that he cut it further, and ran for the door still screaming. He opened it, but before he could get out the woman's arm rushed past his face and pushed the door shut. Jack turned and ran blindly into the kitchen. The kitchen door was bolted and Jack struggled with the bolt, his shaking fingers unable to undo it. He felt her presence behind him; she was as cold as ice, breathing on his neck and shoulders as she spoke.

"Make love to me now, and we will be together forever," she whispered.

Jack tore away and shoulder-charged the window, ducking his head as the glass shattered. The rotted window frame gave way under his weight, sending him flying into the front garden. Staggering to his feet, he noticed his face was bleeding. He looked around but the ghost was nowhere in sight. "She can't leave the house," he whispered to himself and laughed uncontrollably. He tripped and fell, sending waves of pain up his bleeding arm. Jack made it to the car, and dropped the car keys twice before he managed to unlock the door. When he drove off with screeching tires he made sure not to look in the rear view mirror.

§§§

The estate agent tried the light switch a couple of times. "Seems they cut off the electricity," he said apologetically.

"Never mind," the man said. "I think it's still bright enough to get an idea." He looked around. "Old," he said.

The estate agent agreed. "It has quite unexpectedly come

back on the market," he said. "The previous owner bought it as an investment, but he ran into trouble with his finances and had to sell again. Mind the second step... I'm afraid it's broken."

Spiderface

by Vincent Ngai

The house on a tiny suburban lot was already swarming with cops by the time Ann pulled in. An officer was already at her window before she finished parking. As he approached, she lowered the glass halfway.

"Can I help you?"

"Ann Ranger. Here to see Detective Aiden."

The officer seemed skeptical but picked up his radio and barked, "Get me Detective Aiden."

After a pause, a voice replied through the radio. "Aiden here. Go ahead."

"Someone named Ann Ranger here to see you."

"Send her up." The officer lowered his radio and gestured for Ann to follow.

Ann took a glance above him as she walked in his wake. The white house was spotless, save for the giant hole in the wall of the second floor. Grime surrounded the damage as if

17

the house was bleeding filth, but through it Ann noticed a distinct pattern that reminded her of animal tracks.

Inside, Ann found every room filled with police. An adult couple was in the dining room where an officer was trying to interview them through their barely coherent sobbing. The weeping followed her through the walls as she followed the officer up the stairs.

At the top, a large black man emerged from a bedroom, nodded and said, "Thank you. I'll take it from here."

Ann kept quiet as the officer nodded and started back down the stairs. She noticed an uneasy look on the large man's face that lingered even as he politely offered a handshake, which she accepted.

"Detective Aiden. Thanks for coming."

"Didn't know the police called people like me."

"Our mutual acquaintance likes to keep your people… open to mine."

"Seems so," Ann muttered as she followed him into the bedroom.

The detective stepped aside to give her room to enter and continued, "Chief told me about you. Didn't buy it till recently."

"Same here, actually."

"Yeah? What changed your mind?"

Ann looked at him for a moment before quickly answering, "Long story."

The large man leaned back against the door frame and asked, "You really who we sent for? Don't even look like you're out of high school."

"I'm twenty three," Ann said, resisting the urge to roll her eyes.

"Guess puberty short-changed you."

She grunted dismissively, making another mental reminder to herself that one day she should get around to buying more professional clothes than the loose, ratty jeans, her tank top, and that black trench coat that made her look smaller than she already was. Maybe then they'd take her more seriously.

She eyed the room as she made her way to the middle of it. There were dirty clothes and sports memorabilia scattered everywhere, in addition to some choice bits of women's lingerie. Dried blood caked the bed and floor in a splatter that led out the hole in the wall.

"What are the facts?" she asked, feeling like she'd seen too many bodies that week already.

"The parents were out for the weekend and their son and his girl decided to have some alone time. By the time the parents came home early this morning, the kid was gone and the girl was in pieces. The weird part is that no one noticed until the mom came to the bedroom."

"No one noticed a huge hole in the wall?"

"They say it looked fine until she touched something. Next thing everyone knew, there was a giant hole and a dead girl. As far as we can tell, some big animal came in through the wall, killed her, and dragged the boy off. Not that anyone buys that story, which is why you're involved." His skeptical expression suggested he hadn't been the one to make the call.

Ann closed her eyes for a moment and took a quiet,

meditative breath. As her mind calmed, her body felt like it became transparent. She felt a decisive chill to the air, but as far as she could tell that was just the breeze coming in through the gaping hole in the wall. Ann opened her eyes and moved towards the hole—debris crunching under her sneakers with every step—and knelt down to examine the damage. There were several gashes she was certain were claw marks.

"No one heard anything?" she asked.

"Not a damn soul. Everyone we questioned insisted they heard and saw nothing. After the second time this happened, the chief had me call you."

"Second time?" Ann turned back to him and let her senses dull back to normal.

"Yeah. Been a couple of incidents like this. We had some kids at school questioned. All we're getting is some weird story about a bunch of them having the same dream. Somehow it lets them know they're a target."

"What are they dreaming about?"

"A woman, or so I'm told. Not sure actually. I'm told you people can... sense things. Sense anything?"

"No. I don't think there's anything here to sense."

The detective snorted and shook his head. "Almost had me thinking we just hired a kid consultant from the secret Catholic Wizard School."

Ann swept the room one more time but felt nothing new. She turned back to Aiden and asked, "What about those kids you mentioned? Got any I can talk to?"

"There is one who came straight to me. He says he's sure he's the next target."

"Take me to him."

§ § §

Aiden led her just two blocks down to another house squeezed onto a tiny lot. The detective knocked on the door while Ann looked around the neighborhood and let her thoughts drift. Once again, there was a sudden cold breeze— one far stronger than before.

"Ann?"

The voice was garbled and unfamiliar, which snapped her to attention. When Ann opened her eyes the neighborhood was dark and covered in ice. The rotting corpse of a Chinese girl stood in front of her, dressed in the stained remains of a pink dress. It glared at her with shriveled, blank eyes. She snarled with a ripped mouth filled with black nails for fangs and lunged. Ann stepped back and her hand dove into her coat for her gun where it rested in a shoulder holster.

"Ann!" Aiden's outraged voice broke through, and suddenly Ann was back in a normal neighborhood with the detective and a woman at the now open door giving her shocked looks. She froze in place as her mental image of the dead girl faded. When she was certain she was back in reality, Ann took her hand off her sidearm and rubbed her face.

"What the hell is wrong with you?" Aiden asked.

"Sorry. I… thought I saw something."

The large man nodded slowly, though something in his eyes suggested that conversation wasn't over, before he turned to the other woman and flashed his badge. "Mrs. Laurence? I'm Detective Aiden. We need to ask your son a few questions."

"Is he in trouble?"

"That's what we need to find out."

The woman nodded slowly and replied, "I'll go get him."

As soon as she left, Aiden glared at Ann and hissed, "What was that about? Do they train you to draw your damn gun on civvies in Catholic Wizard School?"

"I sensed something. Something big," she muttered, rubbing her forehead.

Aiden opened his mouth to respond, but before he could Mrs. Lawrence returned with a teenage boy. He was about a head taller than Ann and dressed in a loose t-shirt and shorts. His scraggly red hair was a greasy mess, and he looked too thin and utterly exhausted. His eyes had the haunted look of someone that was too terrified to sleep.

Ann stepped forward and asked, "What's your name, kid?"

"Kevin."

"I'm Ann and this is Detective Aiden. We understand you've been having some bad dreams, Kevin. Same dreams the other murdered kids had. What can you tell me about them?"

"You're a police officer?" Mrs. Laurence squawked, unbelieving.

Ann sighed, "No. I'm from the church."

Kevin's eyes suddenly widened with hope. "You're a Martyr, then?" he asked breathlessly. Though rather startled, Ann kept her expression neutral and merely nodded.

"Kevin?" his mother asked.

"It's okay, Mom. Lemme talk to her."

Mrs. Laurence gave them a concerned look, but eventually she nodded, "Shout if you need me."

Once she was gone, Ann looked at Kevin, her voice dropping to a harsh whisper. "How do you know about us?"

"My grandfather was one and he used to tell me all about you guys. Sounded like something out of a movie. Ever since this started happening though I never believed him. And now you're here, so I guess he was right."

"Well, he was and I'm here to help you. So what's going on?"

Kevin rubbed his hands together nervously. "About a month ago a kid in my class started having dreams about this creepy woman we call Spiderface. She comes twice, and only if you have a girlfriend. Third time, the guy disappears and the girl is killed. At first we thought it was just an isolated thing, but then other guys started talking about having it too."

"And now you've had this dream?"

"Twice."

"Hold still," Ann said and stepped forward. She placed a hand on Kevin's head, closed her eyes, and let her mind expand once more. This time the cold shot through her so fast that she hissed in surprise and pulled back.

"What is it?" Aiden asked as his eyes went wide, fear filling them.

"A curse, and a big one," Ann replied while she rubbed her hand.

What color remained in Kevin's face drained. "C–can you cure me?"

"Not that easy. I'm guessing a demon put that on you. Some kind of psychic spell that needs time to grow, which might be why she has to visit three times. Are you dating anyone right now?"

The boy rubbed his arms like he felt something crawling on him. "For about a day before I got my first dream. My girl, Judy, thought breaking up would make it stop, but it didn't. It's like Spiderface just knows."

"So she goes after you even if you break up?"

"Well, not Brian. After his first dream, he and Christie broke up so he started dating her sister. She's the one who got killed."

"We were just at Brian's house, actually. He only moved in recently too. Before that a girl lived there who was also called Spiderface," Aiden said.

Kevin shifted uncomfortably and murmured, "You mean Sharon? Sharon Mabel? I knew her. She had this huge acne mark on her face that looked like a spider. Plus she was kinda fat so she was always getting picked on. Last year, she hung herself."

Ann sighed, "Good job."

Kevin raised his hands defensively. "Judy and I tried to

talk her out of it! Besides, this Spiderface doesn't look anything *like* Sharon! We just call her that because some of the guys said they saw spiders on her face."

"What do you think, Ann? Dead girl coming back for revenge?" the detective asked sardonically. The police always called them but never actually wanted their help.

"Seems that way. Where was she buried?"

"There's a cemetery on the west side of town, near an orchard. She had family living near there. Grandparents, I think." The detective held his chin in thought. "They're pretty old so they don't go out much."

"Let's check that out then." Ann turned to leave, but suddenly felt something tug at her sleeve. She found a panicked Kevin tightly holding her.

"What about me? I haven't slept for two days! If I fall asleep again she'll come for me! Maybe even Judy, too! What are we supposed to do?"

Ann opened her mouth, but no words came out and her mind stalled. It was a good question. When she looked over at Aiden, he shrugged and offered, "Maybe you two should date?"

She stared at him. "What?" Her voice was flat and the expression on her face must have been rather empty because he backed up a step.

"That might get Spiderface off of Judy's back and bring her right to you."

The idea made perfect sense, but Ann wanted to protest anyway for reasons that did not become clear until she took another look at Kevin.

"How old are you, kid?"

"Sixteen."

"I'm sure most people would buy *you* being seventeen at least," Aiden chuckled in a manner that wasn't entirely friendly.

"I suppose you have a point," the Martyr sighed. As much as she doubted a fake date would fool a psychic demon, she could think of no alternatives that would allow her to both protect Spiderface's targets and root the demon out at the same time.

The detective started back to the car and said, "I'll get some people to keep an eye on Judy. Just in case." Ann wanted to say something sarcastic about how they'd done a fantastic job protecting Brian and his girlfriend but she bit her tongue. If he was going to help she'd accept it because at the moment she had no choice.

Ann instead turned back to the boy and said, "Kevin, get your mother so we can tell her what we're doing. Then, I guess we should make this official while we check out that grave-yard."

Kevin grinned and muttered, "Great place for a first date." When she shot him another glare indicating she heard him, his smile faded and he quickly added, "So you sure this will work?"

The young woman softened her expression and patted him on the shoulder. Her thoughts briefly went back to a girl standing in the rain as she said, "I won't let anything happen to you, Kevin. I promise."

§ § §

Though Ann understood dating as two people spending time together in an attempt to build a romantic relationship, she doubted he was in any condition to fake any kind of interest in her. The thought of her doing the same, faked or not, sickened her.

Kevin made no objection when she suggested a fast food meal to make their pairing as "official" as Ann could see it becoming and gave her directions to a Wendy's that had just opened for lunch.

Ann fumbled with the receipt as she took the bag from the hair-netted woman at the drive thru window and handed it to Kevin. When she glanced at him, an older, more handsome man with smooth features and black hair tied back in a pony tail smiled at her and took the bag. She drew in a sharp breath as the warmth bled from her body.

"Matt?" Ann whispered incredulously. She blinked twice to try and see if what she was seeing was real. After the second time, Kevin was sitting across from her giving her a puzzled look. Blood rushed back to her face, which she promptly slapped, and she growled, "Damn it."

"You okay?"

"It's the curse. It's got me seeing things since I'm sensitive to this stuff as a Martyr," Ann explained, still blushing as she grabbed their drinks and plunked them into the tray before pulling out of the drive-thru lane. She drove off a bit faster than was technically legal, determined to waste no more time getting to the cemetery.

After a moment, Kevin spoke up, "Do you want to talk about it?"

Her face must have twisted up in some unpleasant way when she looked at him, because he immediately recoiled. The boy turned his gaze out the window, cleared his throat, and added, "U–unless you don't want to."

"Sorry. I just haven't really talked to anyone since I left home years ago. Not exactly something I can just share with a stranger, you know?"

Kevin's voice became more confident and he relaxed, leaning back into his seat, "Sharon was the type to keep things bottled up, too. I don't think it's a good idea, and sometimes it helps if the listener doesn't know you. Besides, dates are where we're supposed to get to know each other better."

At a light, Ann stopped to glance at Kevin as he shoved some fries into his mouth and offered the rest to her. A slight smirk briefly formed on her lips as she helped herself to a handful and munched down on them. After she finished she asked, "Ever make a promise you couldn't keep?"

"Like I said, everyone picked on Sharon so she had no friends or anything. One day, I just decided to talk to her. We became friends and I promised to help her if she ever needed it, but I guess I wasn't there enough for her." Kevin sighed and slouched in his seat, his shoulders drawing up defensively.

The light turned green and they drove through onto a straightaway. Ann fished for more fries while letting her thumb guide the wheel as she said, "I can relate to that. I promised my best friend we'd always be friends no matter what. Then I left her over something stupid and by the time I realized it, it was too late."

"What happened to her?"

The Martyr shifted uncomfortably for a moment before she finally muttered, "Demons."

"They do this kind of thing often or what?"

"Incidents are actually rare. Most people can go their whole lives and not see a thing. When they do happen, though, it can be a disaster. And even when we stop it there's no evidence to prove anything."

"That's why you guys can't just go to the President and say, 'hey, demons are real and killing people so we need some paranormal police to stop them?'"

"Exactly."

Silence settled between them as the busy stores that cluttered the road eventually gave way to a patchwork of forests and open spaces. The change in scenery stirred more memories Ann would have preferred to have remained undisturbed in the back of her mind.

"So why are they here?" Kevin asked.

"Sad thing is, demons start here. They used to be human."

"Really?"

"Demonic magic can be very appealing to desperate or greedy people. Accepting it is always a choice, but doing so allows the worst part of you to take over. After that… even the best intentions just become mindless destruction."

Kevin looked down in thought and asked, "Can demons turn back into people?"

"Yes. If they redeem themselves"

"How do they do that? Just say 'I'm sorry?'"

Ann shook her head and jabbed herself in the chest with a finger as she said, "Has to come from in here. The change has to be real and you got to act on it or you're just lying to your-self."

Silence settled in again for a minute before Kevin asked, "... So you think Sharon is Spiderface?"

"Yeah."

"Can anything be done for her?"

"I'm not sure. It's up to her really."

"What about me? I never asked for this curse." He sounded scared and defensive.

"You're just collateral to demons, but don't worry. I said I wouldn't let anything happen to you and I'm going to keep that promise."

She could feel a surge of warmth and relief coming from his direction as he smiled at her. "Thanks."

Ann returned his smile and gave him another pat on the shoulder. "No problem."

§§§

An old metal arch held up by old chunks of weathered stone marked the cemetery's entrance. A single main road split the place neatly in half, while smaller branching arms divided the rest into neatly organized plots. To her right, in the distance beyond the cemetery, Ann spied a single farmhouse hunkered on a grassy hill and felt a cold so intense that she involuntarily shivered.

Kevin was not affected, but he noticed and asked, "What's up?"

"I think we're getting close."

When she felt the cold intensify to an almost bone-chilling level, she stopped the car. "Stay here," she said as she opened the door to the car.

"Is it a good idea for us to split up?" Kevin yawned, putting his hand over his mouth. He was exhausted, though fear was keeping him moving. However, it was obvious that the energy from fear was starting to run out.

"We may not have a choice if you can't stay awake. I should be able to tell if she's coming but…"

Despite the summer-warm breeze that blew over her skin as she stepped from her car, Ann could still feel a piercing cold oozing from the graves she passed. She pulled off her trench coat and left it on the driver's seat, revealing a harness with two holsters situated beneath her arms with semi-automatics in them. Her belt sported loaded magazines in pouches, and a combat knife occupied a sheath on her right thigh. Finally, Ann fished out a teal scrunchie from her pocket and used it to wrangle her hair back and out of her face.

She followed the feeling up a small hill, passing a host of unremarkable graves. After a few feet, she shivered again and found her eyes drawn to a grave labeled "Sharon Mabel" at her feet. The plot looked reasonably recent, though undisturbed. Ann knelt down and ran her hand over the grass. The blades were soft and cool to the touch, which seemed authentic enough... Except, she remembered, it was hot today and she was directly under the sun. She ran her hand over some grass beside her. It was warm and dry.

Ann put her hand on the cool grass again and reflected on Kevin's gratitude and concern, focusing those feelings inside into a warm sensation that filled her. She imagined the warmth going to her hand, through her skin, and over the ground. The grass instantly collapsed in as if growing on a thin layer of dirt over an empty chasm. The fragments dissolved into mist and vanished into the dark, yawning pit below.

The Martyr peered down at the now-open grave, noticing that the coffin's cover was open and the coffin was devoid of a corpse. Suddenly, an intense, electric chill shot up her spine as a heavy fog abruptly closed over the yawning hole and swallowed her feet. She lifted her head and turned to look back towards Kevin and the car. She realized that the fog had grown so thick in those swift moments that it had swallowed the bright, midday sun. A woman's voice echoed in the distance, raised in gentle song.

Hush little baby, don't you cry. Mama will make sure that you never die. Turning around again, Ann saw a vast wall of fog thicker than the rest drifting across everything like a devouring mass. In what was still visible of the other section of the graveyard, she saw a tall, thin figure emerging and approaching the car where Kevin was sleeping.

So sleep, little baby, and don't feel blue. Mama's gonna make all your dreams come true. Ann whipped out her keys and hit the alarm several times but nothing happened. She drew one of her pistols, flipped off the safety, and started dashing back for the car.

And if you dream of love so true, Mama's gonna bring your prince to you. When she reached the vehicle, the figure had come near enough for the Martyr to see a woman's shape. The remote lock still didn't respond, so she jammed her keys into the manual one. It refused to give, as if the lock was just a solid piece of metal. Growling, Ann slammed hard on the glass with her fist and screamed, "Kevin! Wake up!"

And if your dreams are filled with hate. Kevin did not stir, so Ann pointed her gun at the backseat window and fired twice. A cloud-like burst of safety glass appeared, punching open a hole in the window, causing the rest to splinter, collapse, and give her room to reach in and open the door from the inside.

Then Mama's gonna take those whores to their fate.

Something heavy landed on the car and Ann looked up to see a massive set of hairy mandibles barely a foot away from her face. She lifted her gun to fire at it, but a long limb swept in from her right and casually swatted her off her feet. Ann felt the air rush out of her as she was lifted off the ground and sent flying down the road. Her back hit the earth with a bone-jarring thud. She gasped in pain, fighting to get her breath back, while lifting her head to see what hit her.

Climbing down her car was a giant spider that looked as if it had grown out of a man's body. The skin of a large human male stretched tightly over its bloated form, giving it the strange appearance of a fat man with long, bony limbs crawling low to the ground dragging its bulk down the slope of the car's windshield. The legs had been reshaped out of the man's limbs, ripping each in half and each one ending in claws of twisted bone. Instead of a head, there was merely a bloody neck stump where the mandibles, belonging to no creature on Earth, looked as if they had chewed open a hole to eat through. Looking at the grotesque creature, the only name Ann could conjure up was "skincrawler" and so that was what she decided to call it.

Ann climbed to her feet and lined up her sights with the center of the monster's "mouth." A heavy shot thundered out of her gun, but in the split-second it took her to bring her weapon back down from the recoil, the monster was to her left and the shot hit nothing but pavement. She hadn't even seen the thing *move*, let alone had the ability to adjust her aim for it.

The skincrawler pounced at her, throwing itself through the air with surprising speed. Ann twisted her body to her left and stepped back, narrowly avoiding being hit. A claw sliced through her shirt, leaving a large tear over her stomach but only lightly grazing her skin. She completed her turn, brought her hands together around her piece, and aimed while the demon was still scrambling to face her again. This time, the .45 hollow-point struck one of its leg joints and it exploded in shower of bone and yellow ichor. The creature stumbled onto the pavement shrieking and scratching at the ground wildly with its remaining legs. Ann put one more shot into its "face" and the creature stopped moving completely.

From behind, Ann could hear the lullaby end. She spun around and found a tall, thin woman with gray, withered skin smiling down at her with dry lips and a single, gaping eye glaring down at her, the rest of the woman's face hidden behind a curtain of black hair. Ann thrust her piece into the towering demon's face and fired. The face blurred and a hole appeared as if she had just shot through the fog itself and soon settled back to normal.

A curse was about to escape Ann's lips, but long, thin fingers slithered around her neck, cutting her off. Her gun was taken away and crushed by another withered hand. Ann clawed furiously at the demon's grip, but could only touch her own neck as she was lifted off the ground. Spiderface made an echoing chuckle and casually tossed Ann aside.

The Martyr flew across the street and landed flat on the grass. Pain stunned her senses as if her body became dead weight, but she managed to lift her head and see Spiderface moving towards the car. The Martyr closed her eyes and began to concentrate, calling up a warmth within her that soothed her pain and lightened her battered body.

When she opened her eyes, the skincrawler came bursting back into view overhead, coming straight down towards her. She pushed hard against the ground, going into a desperate roll. The shockwave of the beast landing slapped her entire body, but she was clear and the monster seemed to knock the wind out of itself. Ann rose to her feet and drew her knife.

The first lesson she was ever taught about a Martyr's power was that it all came from within, but could be channeled to anything the user held. Bullets were no longer part of her weapon the moment they left the barrel and thus could carry no enchantments, but a knife never had to leave her hand. Most Martyrs were trained in knife play for just that reason. Ann flipped the blade into a reverse grip and drove it down into the demon's body while pouring all her efforts into a single thought of protecting Kevin. Golden light lit the creature from within with a fiery glow that erupted out of its every orifice. The skincrawler fell to the ground in a smoking heap of burnt out flesh.

Ann staggered back, but caught herself, gasping for breath. Frantically, she looked over towards the car. Kevin had emerged from the car and was standing, dumbly gawking up at Spiderface with glazed eyes.

"Kevin!" the Martyr shouted.

He responded, but not to her. "Sharon is waiting for me?" Spiderface bowed her head in acknowledgment, her face vanishing in the shadows cast by her hair.

Ann flipped her knife back into a forward grip and raced towards them, but the demon turned towards her. From behind the towering woman's back, a long, black spider leg emerged and spat out something stringy and white that hit

Ann in the chest and sent her back to the ground again. She groaned half from her pain and half from pure frustration as she grabbed at the substance on her and held up thick, sticky webbing.

Suddenly, Spiderface was looming over her with that single, unblinking eye staring down at her with hate, but smiling like a child at play. Ann saw something shuffle under the curtain of hair as it was draped over her until all she could see was darkness.

§ § §

Something wet touched her face, and Ann realized it was raining. She opened her eyes and found herself on a street in a quiet, familiar neighborhood. The only other soul with her was a short, scrawny girl with blonde hair tied into a pair of braided pony tails draped over her chest. "Mary?" Ann asked, fumbling with the name for a moment in sheer confusion.

"'Allo, Ann," the girl said in a thick British accent as she offered a cheerful smile despite the sadness in her eyes. She gestured to the house closest to them—a small, two-floor house with yellow sidings and a brown roof that Ann recognized as her own—and added, "We should probably go inside. Everyone's waitin' and you don't want to catch cold, love."

Ann felt an itch on her throat and scratched it absent-mindedly while her mind wrangled with the feelings that were swirling around in her chest. Half of her felt that she was home, all was well, and that she should follow the girl's advice. The other half rejected everything the first part thought was perfectly logical, though she couldn't quite pinpoint why. "Who's waiting for me?"

"Everyone, love! All our friends, your parents, and of course, Matt." Mary chuckled teasingly at the mention of the last name.

The pain in Ann's neck began to throb as if trying to break through her trachea. She brought her hands up to her face and tried to rub away her confusion. Somewhere, behind the pain, she vaguely remembered another time and place far from here.

"Ann? Is something wrong?" the girl asked, her voice light and gentle.

Ann scratched at her throat as she muttered, "This isn't right. I shouldn't be here."

"Don't be silly. You promised we'd always be together and that you'd never leave me, remember?" Mary chuckled and offered her hand.

The voice in Ann's head told her everything was fine: Mary was her best friend, she had promised her, and there was nothing stopping her from keeping that promise. Her mind was convinced enough to try and block out any other possibilities, but there was one vague thought that Ann snatched through the tension headache that she was starting to feel clawing up the back of her neck: she *had* promised, but she *did not keep it*.

"But I did leave. Years ago."

"Well now you won't have to. Come with me, Ann."

Suddenly, Ann felt a burst of clarity that banished her headache and left her with a cold realization of where she really was. She took a step back away from the girl who looked like Mary and snapped, "No. This isn't real. You're not Mary!"

The other girl's faced twisted into a scowl and she lowered her face until her bangs fell over her eyes, obscuring them completely. Her words came out in a venomous hiss, "You're going to abandon me? Again?"

"Don't hand me any of that bullshit! You aren't Mary and this isn't real!" Ann reiterated.

The girl lifted her head, revealing lidless sockets of darkness in the place of her eyes. Her cheeks burst apart in a bloody shower as skincrawler mandibles ripped free. The creature uttered a screech that merged its voice with Mary's and lunged at the Martyr. Ann responded by ducking and coming up with an uppercut to the monster's gore-smeared "jaw".

Then she found herself on her back with the sun beating down on her face while an intense pain bore down on her throat. Something heavy and sticky held her down, but she had one free arm to grab at her neck. Her hand closed around a fat brown spider and tore it from her neck. It screeched at her with a high-pitched whine and Ann snarled in response, tightening her grip and silencing it with a pulpy crunch.

She tore at the webbing on her other arm frantically, freeing enough of it herself to rip away the rest. Once she'd finally disentangled herself, Ann put all her strength into sitting up and broke free. Blood dripped from the bite on her neck, but her throat seemed to work fine and the blood flow was reasonably minimal. The Martyr dragged herself to her feet while steadying herself on a gravestone and forced her bleary gaze to sweep the area. Oddly, she saw no signs of battle nor did she see any demons, including the one she had killed. Her scan of the area stopped on the farmhouse in the distance where she once more felt a cold feeling that she had no more doubts about.

§ § §

A weak, rusted iron fence was all that separated the cemetery from the farm. Ann drove straight through, sending her car up the hilly rise towards the house. The terrain bumped her car along, smoothing out only when she reached the winding dirt path that ran all the way down the hill. She slid the car to a stop on the path in front of the house, kicking up a cloud of dust.

The Martyr stepped out and swapped in a fresh clip from her belt into her spare piece and chambered a round. She still had her knife, and the bandage she'd hastily applied to her neck seemed to be holding. Ann took another meditative breath and the pain from earlier dulled to the point where she could ignore it while her energy returned. She gripped her gun tightly in one hand and her knife in the other as she marched towards the house.

An old, locked door barred her path into the house. She gave the door a hard kick near the knob, causing rotten wood to splinter and the door to cave inward. It creaked open to reveal a hallway covered in thick, dusty spider webs. The cold sensation she felt on Kevin and at the graveyard was everywhere, threatening to smother her senses, but also cementing the fact that she was in the right place.

Ann moved with slow, deliberate steps, keeping as quiet as she could. Passing by what used to be a living room and a den, but was now thick with webbing, Ann got the impression of a giant nest and thought back to the skincrawler. Then she heard one hiss behind her. *Bingo*, she thought.

She spun around and saw one emerging from the living room she passed, but before she could train her pistol on it, another hiss came from above. A second creature dropped down from a hole in the ceiling just a foot away from her. Surrounded in the narrow hall, she couldn't out maneuver them, but then again, she didn't have to.

The closest skincrawler reared up in a fearsome display before slashing down with its claws. Ann wasted no time and stepped towards it, stabbing her knife just under its maw. She sent in a surge of holy energy—though less than before—that seared the creature's insides before firing at where she suspected its heart and lungs would be if it still had any similarities to human anatomy. Much to her satisfaction, the demon stopped moving and she stepped away. The corpse ripped free of her knife and hit the ground with a wet thud.

Ann turned in time to see the other one leap at her, but

was already moving to counter well before that. Drawing in a sharp breath and focusing her power, Ann thrust with her knife. The skincrawler landed on the blade and was repelled by a burst of golden fire, sending it tumbling backwards. While the demon staggered, Ann put its "face" in her sights. The first shot sent it sprawling further back, but still it screamed at her. She fired again and again, each shot steadily reducing the demon's defiance into dying gasps. When her gun clicked emptily, the skincrawler finally fell to the floor and stayed there.

Ann paused to let out a sigh of relief while she pushed the magazine release and let the mag drop to the ground at her feet. Instantly, she regained her focus and slammed in the last clip from her belt.

A kitchen as green and overrun as the rest of the house was at the end of the hall. When she entered, Ann noticed a series of portraits decorating a cleaner patch of wall that showed the progressive aging of a married couple along with their growing family. A few photos included a chubby girl with a noticeable acne spot on her face. Under one picture of the girl alone was a dusty sticky note that read: *We thought our family secret would die with us, but for you, Sharon, we will use it one more time.*

Suddenly, a muffled voice singing to the tune of "Hush Little Baby" came from above. Ann whipped around, looking for a way up, and spotted a staircase to her left across the kitchen. She barreled up the stairs that wound to her left and into a narrow hallway that wrapped around the shape of the kitchen. The first door on her right was a large bedroom. Inside, she found the room covered in enough webs to reshape the room into a round cave. The severed heads of several young men hung in the webbing with pained smiles stuck on their faces.

In the back of the room was a dirty old bed with the decayed corpse of a girl resting with her hands crossed against her chest. Kevin stood on one side of the bed, his fingers lovingly caressing the dead girl's cheek, a dreamy smile plastered on his young face. On the other side of the bed, her mouth stretched in a dark smile, stood Spiderface. Ann trained her gun on the demon and shouted, "Kevin! Move!"

Kevin did not seem to hear her, but Spiderface was already turning. Ann found that gaping eye glaring angrily at her while her dry, flaking lips twisting into a wide scowl. Ann fired a shot, but the bullet passed through Spiderface once more.

"Damn it! What the hell are you?"

Spiderface's lips moved, but it was Mary's voice that said, "I'm your friend."

She slowly began walking towards Ann and spoke again, this time in another girl's voice. She pointed a long finger at Kevin and said, "I am his friend. I want to be with him."

The demon clutched her long hands to her chest and an older woman's voice cried, "I told her she'd always be my precious little angel, but I let her die!"

The moment the demon stopped speaking she returned to her drifting posture with arms slightly spread. Ann reigned in her anger, nodding slowly. "You're just Sharon's dream, not Sharon, aren't you."

The demon's lips twisted into a scowl and the girl's voice—Sharon's, Ann presumed—snarled, "Everybody hates me because I'm *ugly*! It's not enough for them to be pretty and have dates and friends! No! They have to rub it in! They have to remind me that I'll *never* have what they have!"

Spiderface suddenly curled into herself and whimpered, "I couldn't take it anymore. But I remembered there was one boy who was nice to me. He gave me a present for my birthday. He was the only one who bothered to remember."

Ann stole a glance past Spiderface to where Sharon lay, strangely peaceful, as if she were asleep instead of dead. Clutched in the girl's withered hands was a crudely made dream catcher.

"It was supposed to keep away bad dreams, but I heard you could wish for good dreams on them. I thought if I could just dream about having friends or being in love, then go to sleep forever, I could be happy forever."

Ann followed Spiderface's movements as the demon pointed at one of the grisly trophies on the wall, then tapped her own head afterwards. Spiderface pointed at Ann and dragged a finger across her own throat.

"I get it. You steal dreams from the guys and kill the girls as some kind of wish-fulfillment," Ann murmured, unimpressed. Once more, she stole a glance at Sharon's body and the dream catcher. Her arm snapped out and she took aim.

Spiderface let out a monstrous shriek and eight black spider legs swarmed out from behind her back. A shot of webbing slammed into Ann's wrist, throwing her arm back and causing her shot to go wide. The other legs spat more strands and brought Ann down to the floor.

The demon swooped in and hovered over the Martyr, pulling her hair back to reveal the full horror of her face. Blood-red blisters blossomed from a split cheek, sealing the eye above with the swollen sores. The blisters cascaded down the cheek to the corner of the demon's mouth. One of the sores squirmed for a moment before the flesh parted and a fat, glistening spider wiggled free.

Ann pulled hard to free her hand holding her gun, but black spider legs came down and impaled her hands, pinning her completely. Her fingers reflexively tensed and she and heard her gun go off, followed by Kevin screaming. Beyond Spiderface, Ann saw the boy clutching his shoulder where her shot grazed him. He looked quite awake and screamed at the sight of Spiderface's room.

"Kevin, the dream catcher! Break the dream catcher!" she yelled over his screeching.

Kevin seemed bewildered, but quickly understood what she meant. Spiderface flew across the room like smoke in the wind and stopped between him and Sharon's body, causing the boy to recoil with a frightened gasp.

The demon spoke in Sharon's voice, "Wait! Don't hurt me, Kevin!"

"Sharon?"

As she struggled to free herself, Ann shouted, "It's a trick! The demon is a parasite! It's using her!"

Spiderface hovered over the terrified teenager and clasped her hands together. Sharon's voice pleaded, "I thought you were my friend! You *promised!*"

Ann pulled hard against the webbing, stretching but not breaking it. Before her, Kevin was looking back and forth between Sharon's body and Spiderface, shaking with uncertainty. "Please, Kevin. Don't you want me to be happy?" The girl continued to try and get his attention.

Slowly, as Kevin settled his gaze on Spiderface, his breathing calmed and he regarded the demon with saddened eyes. He lowered his head, clenched his fists, and said "I do want Sharon to be happy. That's why I can't leave her like this."

Ann put all her strength, magical and mundane, into one arm and pulled. The webbing finally snapped loose and her arm came free, followed by enough of her body to sit up. She saw Spiderface's body explode into mist and Kevin became visible through the swirl. The demon whipped around and reached out, its fingers slithering around Kevin's arms, and pulled him back. Another blister burst, dripping a spider down onto the demon's shoulder.

The Martyr knew shooting the little spider was too risky, shooting Spiderface was useless, and she couldn't see the dream catcher. Instead, she aimed at Sharon's corpse and fired, striking the foot. Spiderface screamed like never before as the lower part of her burst apart and faded away and her form became transparent. Kevin ripped free of the demon's ghostly fingers and seized the dream catcher in his fist.

There was a barely audible snap, and blinding light exploded from the boy's hand. Ann shut her eyes as a storm of wind whipped around them. She heard Spiderface's scream dissolve under the roar of the wind as the rest of her bindings tore free. She tried to open her eyes, but the light was too much.

The wind threw Ann against the wall, her head striking the hard surface with a brain-jarring thunk and then, just as abruptly, both the light and the roaring wind vanished. Experimentally, she opened her eyes to find the room was filled with chunks of debris, though all evidence of Spiderface had evaporated. Sharon's body was missing as well; all that remained was a large burn mark on the bed. Beside the bed, Kevin was trying to force himself to his feet with limited success. Though Ann had little strength left herself, she called up one final surge so she could stand and stagger over to help Kevin.

"Are you okay?" she asked as she strained to help the boy to his feet.

He nodded and groaned, "I think so. What happened?"

The Martyr let her thoughts drift for a moment and found the cold chill was gone. There was no warmth or feeling of any kind. The room was devoid of any spiritual energy at all, leaving a scar that no one could see but would linger for a long time.

"It's over. Spiderface is dead," she sighed and let him go. Ann flexed her wounded hands which hurt, but would recover. Beside her, Kevin opened his hand which held the remains of the dream catcher.

He looked at her and asked as she took the pieces from him, "What was she?"

"A dream made into a curse."

"But how? I made that dream catcher in grade school." Kevin sounded confused and horrified.

"I saw a note downstairs. Her grandparents must have known some black magic and changed it themselves. Probably to bring her back to life, but I guess Spiderface killed them, too."

"But all they wanted was for her to be happy."

"Like I told you, even the best intentions can become mindless destruction when demons get involved," Ann replied and pocketed the remains of the dream catcher while the boy stared sorrowfully at the burnt bed.

"So what do you think happened to Sharon?"

"I don't know." Kevin sighed at her response, but nodded as Ann led him out the door.

"I take it we're breaking up now, right?" he muttered around a yawn.

"I think that's a pretty fair bet."

Shaman

by Ryan E. Miller

The man was not a hermit by choice but out of necessity. His first name was Doug; his last name no longer mattered. What few living relatives he shared that name with had all but forgotten him, and it was probably better that way. Doug had adapted to his lifestyle out of necessity. He did not think others would adjust quite as well. He lived a sparse monk-like existence on a meager government disability check. The only time he would leave his secluded patch of forest was once a month when he drove into town for supplies. On each trip he felt the eyes of all the "normal" people piercing his soul, and he could hear them muttering as he passed by. Over the years he'd become something of a local curiosity. However, those judgmental gazes were not from the eyes he really had to worry about.

Doug lived in an old shack miles out in the woods, nestled near the river bottoms of the Ozarks in a secluded valley. Any would-be guest to his home would first notice fish hooks tacked to the walls in plain view in every room. On these fish hooks hung strips of bacon. The strips of raw flesh lent a thick, meaty odor to the cabin's interior. If asked about the peculiar and almost obsessive ritual, the most explanation he would give would be a shrug. The wooden floors of his home were gritty with large granules of salt, which he used a hand-cranked yard fertilizer to dispense in massive quantities. Various herbs hung in tied bundles over every door: tobacco, lady slipper, and blue skullcap. These habits were essential to his survival, though his self-taught rituals seemed to most like mad, paranoid activities. A cause-effect relationship was not readily apparent to anyone but Doug, and he didn't seem inclined to explain. He had been labeled "clinically insane" by his doctors, whom he visited a few times a year out of venomous necessity. But he knew that he was quite sane, no matter what any "doctor" said. Doug had learned over the years that he was not, in fact, insane, but rather that he was a man under siege.

Shadows always crept into Doug's little valley a few hours before nightfall, cast by the surrounding hills. The nighttime chorus of crickets and other nocturnal creatures started up, a soothing sound if not for the deepening tension in the air. As the sun slipped below the horizon, *things* started to happen. His carefully prepared signs and alarms would go off, telling him to expect a visit. Tonight, like many other nights, the tension was so powerful that a buzzing filled his ears and the hair on his head felt like it was standing on tiptoe. The bacon on the hooks began to twitch. At first the strips of meat merely jerked sporadically, but soon they began to curl and writhe like worms dipped in alcohol. The herbal wards above the doors would keep the spirit out, as would the salted floor which the spirit simply could not tread upon. But the company the spirit kept, the dead things coaxed halfway back into a mockery of life in the spirit's presence, could cross these barriers. Doug never knew what paths the thing walked to get to the valley, but it would gather up a host of the dead before its arrival; corpses from passing through long-forgotten cemeteries and road kill from slinking across darkened lanes.

Doug readied himself. He didn't bother with conventional weapons—no regular ammunition, nor did he wield such implements as supposed "holy water" or a mallet and wooden stakes. The spirit itself wasn't substantial enough to be physically harmed and its pets were already dead, so most weapons that worked on people had, over the years, shown to be useless. He had the scars to show for it. Instead, he prepared a mixture of salt and the herbs he that knew would at least keep the spirit at bay. Soon the raking of nails (or claws, he considered) on the storm door, the cabin's only entrance, told him that his nightly visitors had arrived. As Doug peered out the window into the moonlit night, he saw the thing glistening in the shadow of the well house outside. "What was it made of?" he wondered. It had the look of snail slime, which seemed to circulate through a structured network of invisible veins and capillaries. The spirit itself had a humanoid shape, the curvature of which was very suggestive of a young woman. The she-thing seemed to glide from the shadows and into the full moonlight, and her host of corpses shuffled from the darkness, pressing their rotting, wormy faces against the window. They didn't enter, though their taunting presence was both nauseating and unbearable.

They had visited him since the time he was a young man—ever since the hunting accident. *A loud ping reverberated through his head, accompanied by unparalleled pain. He lay paralyzed on the ground; his view of the sky was cluttered by tree branches with their leaves in full fall color. His head rested against a tree trunk and he found he could only move his eyes. He saw blood spattered across the bark, running through the grooves that split it like veins and capillaries beneath dark flesh. Then blackness. He dreamed of a woman clothed in a dress of woven moss, her hair the color of fall foliage, dragging herself from beneath the roots of the tree. She expired with her head lying on his chest, bleeding her last all over his body. Not red, but clear and slimy like the trail a snail would leave behind, and sticky, like tree sap.* He still had a deep scar on his forehead where he had been grazed by the bullet. He had spent two weeks in a coma; two weeks of confusing nightmares of the incident. After his long recovery, the haunting began. Through torment, trials, and discovered rituals of practical magic, he'd become a self-proclaimed shaman of sorts, able to keep the she-spirit at bay—if only for another night.

Doug snapped out of his reverie and back into the here and now. The corpses seemed content to slobber graveyard mud and lick the panes of glass, but the spirit seemed to be gathering moonlight, becoming less dim and transparent while gaining luminosity and solidity. This was something new, and it disturbed the man down to the pits of his bones. Doug had learned through experience to deal with her tricks over the years, but over time her approach and tactics had taken on new and varying characteristics. It was as though she was learning and improving the art of torment through experience. The corpses parted like waves as she stepped forward and pressed her semi-solid palm against the window. The pane cracked, and Doug fell over just about every piece of furniture between himself and the far wall as he retreated from the broken glass. It took him more than a moment to regain his composure and to think about what had just happened. It looked like the haunt was learning to manifest herself physically as well. Even she seemed impressed with this newfound gift.

The spirit threw back her head and let out a cackle that sounded like the strangling of a crow. In that same instant her triumphant laugh was cut short as low storm clouds moved in and shrouded the moon, blocking its nourishing light. The laugh turned to a shriek as the spirit grew dim again. This sudden waning of power abruptly robbed her of her fledgling solidity and her glistening mass collapsed and splattered into a puddle of phlegmy slime on the ground. The host of corpses she had raised in her passing crumpled as well. In that instant the spirit had shown Doug both her newfound strength as well as her weakness. Until that night, the spirit's form had never been substantial enough to truly do harm to. Doug was hoping that had changed tonight.

Doug braced himself, choked down his fear, and went outside to investigate the now quiet yard. He examined the small puddle of slime and briefly went back inside to fetch several mason jars. Collecting a large sampling of the goo, he considered what it could have been made of before he finally decided to take Hollywood's advice and label the jar 'Ectoplasm'. He also took tissue samples from the dead and labeled the jars 'Zombie Flesh'. By tomorrow night Doug would need to test the samples to see if any substances or rituals could harm or decompose them. This supernatural harassment had gone on for years, and now he was hoping that he had the means to stop it for good.

The ectoplasm, Doug discovered, actually looked and smelled like the sap of the same type that seeped from a cut in the trunk or branch of a tree in springtime. It had the characteristics of something that would be produced by a plant, yet it also curiously conformed to the traditional notions of the ghostly manifestation ectoplasm that was mentioned in so many ghost stories. So, he surmised, perhaps it was a marriage of both. The spirit, or what he vaguely remembered of it during the hunting accident, had emerged from the tree after it was struck by the very bullet which glanced off his forehead. Perhaps this trauma had linked him to her. Perhaps the link was both from the wounding and from lingering, misplaced blame, as if the undead tree spirit thought Doug was responsible for her death and unwanted rebirth as a haunt. He ruled out trying to communicate or reconcile with her; there was too much of a grudge between them, fueled by years of moves and counter moves in a chess game of contempt. He wasn't as interested in repelling the zombies and risen road kill as he was destroying her, mostly because they seemed to be merely a side effect of her corrupted presence and had never actually attacked him. Doug hoped to rid himself of the haunt permanently, but if he could at least come up with a suitable repellant he would settle for that.

The next day, Doug made a foray to town to buy things to test on the cytoplasmic goo. He was sure he had enough information to formulate a mixture that would stop the spirit. First, there was salt, which he knew was an irritant to her. He stocked up on a fresh supply of rock salt at the local hardware store, who had it on shelves in droves in preparation for winter. Next, he reasoned that if ectoplasm was truly the phlegmy secretion it seemed to be, supernatural or not, it would react as such to various drying agents. So he added many brands of sinus pills with red label warnings on the packages that advised the user to drink lots of fluids with them to prevent dehydration to his list. He also picked up the store brand of the same medicine as Mucinex, which he hoped would break up the ectoplasm the same as if it were phlegm. Finally, based on the smell of the ectoplasm, he rationalized that if the sprit was in any way composed of any type of plant material he might be able to harm it with a powerful herbicide. Doug purchased a large container of an herbicide used for killing shrubs and brush. As Doug shopped, the stares of the "normal" people once again weighed heavily on his shoulders. Today, however, he didn't care. Today he was hoping to become one of them.

Doug returned to the cabin and went diligently to work. First, he crushed up all the pills and mixed them thoroughly with some salt. Then he stirred in the herbicide and mixed the ingredients into a thick paste which he spread on a sheet of wax paper to dry. An hour later he had a white slab of what he hoped would be an effective spirit-killing poison, or at least something that would make her not want to come back. He dropped a small portion of the dried mixture into the jar marked 'Ectoplasm' and watched as the goo dried up and slowly changed color to a dark shade of brown. With this one test, Doug knew he was as ready as he would ever be to face the haunt.

Doug decided on using his shotgun to deliver the toxin. He got the twelve-gauge pump from under the bed and a box of slugs. Using a pocket knife, he cut the end off of each shell and carefully popped the slugs out. The slugs were replaced by chunks of the poison slab, and the ends of the shells were taped over with duct tape, carefully cut into narrow strips so that they wouldn't gum up the barrel of his gun. Locked and loaded, he waited until nightfall, when it was time to hang fresh bacon on the hooks. There was no cloud cover this night and the moon was three quarters full and bright. It would have been an almost holy-looking night except for the fact that the she-spirit would draw power from that glow.

Soon, the bacon began to twitch, then to curl and writhe. But this time its reaction to her approach did not stop there.

The strips started flapping like agitated bat wings, and that feeling he got was much more intense—goose bumps came with the feeling of hair standing on end and a solid chill that sunk to the pit of his stomach. There came the raking of nails on the door, and soon the raking became thumping and pounding. He had pulled the wards down from above the windows and doorframes and swept, mopped, and polished the salt off the floor. This time he would let her onto his battleground for what was, hopefully, a final confrontation. Wood splintered as the outer screen door was ripped off its hinges, followed by a crash as a large, bloated zombie bashed the inner door wide open. The zombie shuffled into the room stiffly, followed by a flattened possum and a mangled deer with only half a shattered antler. The true threat charged into the doorway behind them, and her form was more complete than any other time he had beheld it.

In life she would have been a beautiful dryad, a sylvan sprite left over from an older age long dead save for rare and singular appearances. But now her form was made of amber slime, held together by a skeleton of dead twisted roots and branches. She let out a banshee's wail and came at him as though to tackle him to the floor. Three ear-splitting shots broke off her wail as Doug fired and pumped in rapid succession. Three slugs of concocted poison struck the spirit. One blew her left arm off, the second tore her chest wide open, and the third disintegrated her head. Still, she stumbled forward, fumbling for him. The grip of her right arm was like a vise on his throat as it slammed into him, wrapping her oily fingers through his hair. Another point blank shot sent her flying off of him, giving him time to shoot the three remaining slugs into her now melting form. He knew she was dying at least; the zombies dropped to the floor and the bacon hung limp. In a matter of moments she was nothing but a pile of twigs and goop.

There was a horrible mess to clean up and rotting corpses to rebury, and he would do it gladly.

The Moonstone

Dagger

by Jason Prybylski

Octer. Normally it doesn't get this cold in Detroit until late November. Perhaps it isn't the weather itself, but the night in general: as cold as an ex-lover's glare and twice as unsettling. A crisp, yellow folder hits the old oak desk hard enough to echo off the walls like thunder on a freight train. Sighing, Nicholas sits in the old creaky chair that groans its dissatisfaction from the weight pressed upon it. It isn't that he is heavy—rather that the chair has seen better days over many years. Still, it's comfortable and not worth replacing.

Sitting back for just a moment, Nick reaches to remove the fedora from his head to toss it across to the empty hook on the coat rack beside his already hanging trench coat. Striking the wall, the hat rebounds and lands flat on the floor. Grimacing, Nicholas turns to his desk and looks to the folder the way someone stares at a bomb that's ready to erupt, or a woman who's just declared her love. Skeptical, unsteady, and cautious, Nick decides first to partake in his nightly ritual: liquid leisure.

Moving his hand to the bottom left drawer of the desk before him, Nick slides it open with a dry, wood-on-wood screech. The tall bottle within glistens with its amber colored contents, calling to him with a promise of relief. Reaching in, Nick removes the bottle and glass and sets them on the desk beside the avoided folder. Looking at it again, another sigh slides from his lips. It has only been eight months, but the contents of that folder haunt him still.

An official police sticker decorates the cover. "Officer File: Detective Nicholas Baber" it reads. Below it, "Subject: Former Officer Damen Pierce". Damen. There is a name that will forever burn into the back of his mind, an ember smoldering long after the fire was doused. Not that he wouldn't remember it anyway. They had been in the army together, fighting in the trenches back in France. After almost a decade back home since the fighting had ended, it feels like an eternity has passed.

Closing his eyes, Nicholas takes a moment to try and think it through. It all started the day Damen came to him talking about a strange case that had come across his desk. Like so many of the world's problems, this one started with a dame—a dame that spoke of terrible, recurring nightmares. Nightmares, it seems, are something that this city has in abundance. Opening his eyes, Nick sighs softly as a chill rolls through him, as though having been touched by a ghost. The details of the tale are still somewhat jumbled in his head, and sleep comes rarely these days. The final events still play through his mind in cinematic scenes and manifest themselves in haunting nightmares that plague his nights.

Again reaching for his unlabeled bottle, Nick pops open the cork of his whiskey and pours its contents to the halfway mark of the glass he pulled out of the desk. The smell of it burns his nostrils as it hits the air like a slap to the face after a stolen kiss too bold. It certainly isn't high end liquor, that's for sure, but it also isn't rotgut. Good alcohol has been hard to find ever since prohibition began a few years back, so Nick keeps his stash close to his heart. Lifting the glass, he takes a deep breath before he swallows down a long sip. God, that burns. It's like damnation itself, but the burn quickly turns into that sweet, seductive warmth in the pit of his belly. Soon the soothing rush will swell over him, and his heart will stop racing as he stares the demons of that case in the eye once again.

Setting his glass aside, Nick finally reaches for that folder that is staring him down like a lifer at a new inmate: expectant and unnerving. Sliding it aside, he reaches to pull forth the old typewriter that sits on the edge of the desk and positions it before him. After setting the machine up with paper and a new ribbon, Nick cracks his knuckles and reaches to the keys. The thought strikes him that if he can get it all down on paper, then maybe he will find some surcease from the torment. Perhaps it will be cathartic to unload the demons into a tome of masochistic self-indulgence.

§§§

I doubt anyone will ever read this, which is probably for the best. I write these pages now mostly to get things settled in my heart and in my head, and piece it all together to try and make some sense of what happened. Hopefully, I will have some measure of success in doing so and find myself some semblance of solace in the process. What follows is the tale of my experience eight months ago with Mister Damen Pierce. The information will be comprised of details as I remember them, documented facts from the police file concerning the case, and pages from Damen's journal where he wrote out his experiences during that time.

It was back in March that I received a call from Pierce telling me that he wanted to talk to me about a case he had just started to work on. It was common for us to get together for lunch or coffee just to sit and talk on the day-to-day grind of life that had come in the years after the war. Damen was a good friend, my former partner, and he saved my life back in France. One doesn't usually allow friends of that caliber to just slip away into the ether.

On a sunny Saturday morning, we met up in a small diner in downtown Detroit called "Ashley's Alley". The place smelled of grease and stale coffee, but the prices were sound and the food actually wasn't too bad. The joint wasn't often crowded, so no one was usually sitting close enough to eavesdrop on your conversations.

Past the door was a long counter with stools where most

customers sat for a quick cup of coffee or for some breakfast early in the morning. Beyond that, there was an elegant wooden archway that lead into a dining room that was filled with enamel surfaced tables and chairs. Along the back wall was a row of booths that had been added a few years ago to invite a more family friendly atmosphere. Damen and I normally sat at the furthest booth in the back to avoid the usual hustle and bustle and to have a bit privacy in order to talk business.

I arrived a good thirty minutes before Damen, but he had a tendency to arrive late anyway. He was the only one that worked at his detective agency, and he would often get caught up in his work. I was working with the Detroit police department as a detective at the time, so Pierce often liked to talk to me about his cases and, at times, ask for whatever help I could offer from within the department.

There was no one else in the dining room when I went to sit in our usual spot. The employees knew that I usually only came here when I was meeting with Damen, so nobody bothered to approach me just yet. When he arrived, Damen looked rather ragged and exhausted. It almost seemed as though he hadn't slept for days and was keeping quite busy. After he took his seat across from me, the waitress came by snapping her gum loudly, like fingers keeping to some random beat.

"What can I get'cha?" she asked, holding onto a pair of menus as if we would need them.

"Just coffee for the both of us." It was our usual routine.

The girl only gave me a nod and turned to head to the front with a loud pop of her gum.

Sitting with his head craned low, Pierce didn't have a word to speak at first, so I took it upon myself to break to ice. "You look like you got into a fight with a delivery truck and lost, partner." I smiled slightly, my mouth twitching upwards at the corners.

"No," he groaned through a yawn. "I haven't had much sleep in the last few days. The case I've been on is... rather unique."

The young girl with the bouncing blonde hair and the chorus of snapping fingers between her teeth returned to fill our mugs before leaving us to our peace once more. "Well you said you wanted to talk, so I can only imagine you need something from me again," I commented while adding cream and sugar to my drink.

His reply came in a tired manner, his eyes having finally met my own. "Not so much this time, Nicky. I just want to get this one off my chest so that no one thinks I'm crazy."

Damen's answer intrigued me, to say the least. Most cases that come across his desk are for missing items or women who fear their husbands are unfaithful. "Alright, Pierce," I asked him. "Do you wanna start laying it out to me?"

§ § §

It had been a week earlier that Pierce was in his office downtown. He was clicking away on the keys of the typewriter that sat on his desk writing up notes on the case he had just finished. An average morning, for the most part. The disturbance of such an average day came when there was a knock on his door. "Come on in!" he called, lifting his head from where he sat hunched over his notes. As the door opened, Pierce played it cool. His hands were rested on the keys and his jaw was wired shut. But on the inside, his mind was set to spinning like a carousel as the stranger walked into the room.

She was a bombshell of a dame: buxom, brunette and all things woman. With her silver screen body and face like a goddess from an old Greek tale, the woman was the epitome of elegance and poise. As she looked to Damen, the doll strode across the room making her high-end dress sway and her amber locks bounce. Sitting in the chair across the desk, she turned those golden peepers toward Pierce, instantly setting a blaze to his skin as if some beast straight out of the book of Revelations. "I understand you're a man that has some talent investigating strange matters." She reached to remove a small, gold-lined cigarette case from her bag.

"That's the rumor." Taking up the pocket lighter from his desk, Pierce rose to his feet and leaned over to flick the wick alight for her. The woman leaned forth, placing her cigarette between her lips and dipping the end into the offered flame. Even this simple motion was slow, calculated, and graceful. Once her smoke was lit, she sat back and took a long draw from it before nodding.

"You're my last hope. No one else will believe me, and I need your help."

Damen seated himself again and pushed his typewriter away in order to rest his hands on the desk. "Alright," he nodded. "Let's start with you telling me the problem."

After a long breath, the woman went on to describe her situation. "For the last few months, I have been having such terrible nightmares. In my dreams, I see women being murdered in ways I can only describe as ritualistic. The women would be dressed in white robes and made to lie on an altar as a group of men in masks and red robes chanted and swayed in candlelight."

"Like some manner of cult?" Damen asked her.

"Yes, I believe so. During the ceremony, the head of the cult would step out of the group holding a strange, ornamental knife. The handle was made of some kind of shimmering white stone, like opal or moonstone." The woman paused to take a long draw from her cigarette before she carried on. "At first I passed it all off as an overactive imagination or maybe stress, but these dreams have been going on for months. I can't shake the feeling that there's some truth to what I see in my sleep. I have a sinking, desperate feeling that this isn't just in my mind."

"You see, Mister Pierce, I no longer believe these dreams to be only imagination. I can feel the heat of the candles burning and smell the sweat of the chanters as they sway. I can almost taste the fear of the young girls as that gleaming knife is brought down into their heart." She lowered her eyes to the floor as if reliving some horrid memory. Who could blame her? The cigarette remained dangling in her fingers, burning itself down without living up to its intended use.

"Perhaps it's repressed memories," Pierce suggested. "Traumatic experiences have a tendency to play tricks on our minds. Make us think we see things that aren't there or even forget and hide away the memories of those experiences. Sometimes they come sauntering back. I've seen it myself with some of the men I served with in the war."

The woman shook her head, sighing deeply as she scooted to the edge of her seat leaning in toward Damen. "I believe these girls are real, and I believe there are going to be more. Young women are in danger, Mister Pierce! Please, you have to help me!" she pleaded in a wavering voice as her eyes began to water in frustration.

"Have you spoken to the police?" Pierce asked calmly, trying to keep the air in the room subtle and tranquil.

"I went to them first. They went through the motions of taking down my information and hearing my story, but laughed behind my back and treated me as if I were insane for speaking of it. I was told that there was no evidence and that I needed to see a doctor for my dreams. Afterwards, I was all but shoved out the door!"

As she lifted a hand to her face to hide her tears, Pierce leaned forward and folded his hands upon the desk again like some broker about to lay out the bad news. "Well, Miss… I'm not so sure there's much I can do for you, and my services don't come cheap." He kept his tone steady as he spoke to her.

Lowering her hand from her face, she turned those moistened, dusty eyes his way. "Money is of no concern to me," she sniffled softly. "I can pay whatever it takes. My husband left me everything when he passed."

Sitting back, Pierce nodded to the woman and reached to his stack of blank typewriter paper to slide a sheet over to her along with a quill resting in an inkwell. "Please write down your information so that I can contact you. I'll see what I can do. At the very least I'll look into these murders and see if there are a number of girls missing from anywhere."

She sat forward, taking the quill and began to write. "Oh, thank you so much, Mister Pierce! Thank you!" As she spoke, her eyes softened in visible relief.

"Don't thank me yet. By the way, what do I call you, Miss?" Damen asked as he looked at her expectantly.

"Nomer," she said. "My name is Teresa Nomer."

§ § §

As we sat in the diner, I sipped at my reheated coffee and listened to the tale with genuine interest and concern on my face; to say the very least, the story seemed farfetched and crazy. At the time I believed that Pierce felt the same, but due to his Boy Scout tendencies he had little choice but to act. For some men the need to protect women is instinct. For Damen Pierce it came like thunder.

"So tell me, Pierce..." I sipped at the bad coffee. It was bitter and riddled with old grounds. "What do you need from me?"

With a sigh, Damen looked to me with those weary pools

of deep blue. "Find out who she talked to in the precinct when she came in. I'd like to talk to them and find out if there is any validity to what she told me about getting laughed out of the precinct. Also, if you could help me check to see if there are any instances of girls missing lately, and if there are, find out if there is any connection between them."

I finished the last of my coffee with a grimace before nodding to Pierce. "You know I'll do what I can, partner." I was still convinced that it was a wild goose chase. "Try and get some sleep, if you can. You aren't going to be any good if you're dead on your feet."

Damen reached to rub his hands over his face, offering me a single nod. "I'll try. There's little time. Thanks for your help again, Nicky." He smiled meagerly. "Remember, whenever you're done playing cops and robbers there's room in my office for another desk. You can make your own hours and won't have any superiors breathing down your neck."

With a chuckle, I nodded to Damen. "I'll let you know when the time comes, Pierce. But I'm not ready to toss aside my pension just yet." I grinned at him.

With a handshake and a pat on the shoulder, we parted ways. Once outside, I slipped the fedora back onto my head and shoved my hands into the pockets of my trench coat. I walked with my shoulders hunched, moving against some unblowing wind that ran chills down to my very bones like the shock of a gunshot.

Detroit was known for street crime and was also one of the country's main hubs for bootlegging alcohol. People would wait for the river to freeze over and drive their cars across the ice into Canada to buy liquor. They would then transport it back to the States, where they would run it across the country. But cults, rituals and ceremonial murder? It just seemed so far out of place for the Motor City and so far above the heads of a common flatfoot and a nosy private eye. In any case, as they say, the game was afoot. It was time to find out what truth lay within the dreams of Miss Teresa Nomer.

§ § §

I decided that the first step would be to head back to the department to talk to Beth. Elizabeth Simmons was the clerk in the records department and a friend. If Miss Nomer had indeed gone to speak with the coppers, Beth would know about it.

Once there I made my way back through the department to the stairs that lead to the basement where the records office is located. As I walked through the door, I was greeted by the sight of Beth bent over with her rear toward the door as she rustled and shuffled through folders in one of several open file cabinets. She was yammering to herself like a homeless evangelist. If you talk about hot dames, then Beth had stolen fire from Zeus himself. She had a chassis that was top notch with gams that went all the way up. Her clothes were usually the cat's pajamas, and even the cheaters on her face were stylish and not overbearing to her looks. Glasses on women tend to distract at times, but everything on Beth was copacetic.

"Bethy?" I said, trying to gain her attention. The woman

didn't answer, still talking to herself as though she would be able to answer her own questions. "Bethy, is everything alright?" I watched her with my brow raised in mild concern and interest.

"Oh, applesauce! Where in the world is that... I can't find... huh?" she prattled on, finally turning her head to look back my way. "Oh. Hi Nicky." She lifted upright as she turned to walk over to her desk. "How's it goin', baby?"

"What's eating you?" I pried as she took her seat.

"Oh, nothin'." She waved her hand dismissively and looked up at me with eyes that spoke of days past. We had a thing a couple of years back, and perhaps she still carried a torch. "The big cheese has me all balled up tryin' to figure out this new filing system." She opened her desk to take out her butts. Lifting my pocket lighter, I flicked it on and reached it down for her to lean in and light up. "Thanks Nicky." Beth grinned. "So... what'cha need?" she asked, getting right to the point. I guess I did only talk to her when I needed something these days.

"I'm looking into a caper for a friend and need you to look into something for me. A dame came in not long ago looking for some help with nightmares. I need to know who she talked to here. Also, if you can, find out everything you can about a Miss Teresa Nomer."

Beth gave me a bit of a perplexed look. "Cops for nightmares?" she asked. "The name don't sound familiar, Nicky. But I'll check around for ya'. Might take a while though," she warned, motioning to the disheveled mess behind her.

"Thanks, doll," I replied as I pocketed my lighter.

"So, when we gonna hit that center aisle?" She grinned, taking a pull off her cigarette.

"See ya' soon, Dollface." I winked and headed out the door.

"Oh just ducky," I heard her grumble sarcastically behind me. "You slay me, Baber."

§ § §

Pierce had gone back to his office to gather his things and to jot a few notes into his journal about the current situation. He was only there for a short time before the phone on his desk rang. Lifting the receiver, he already heard frantic breathing on the other end. "Pierce."

"Mister Pierce, I need to see you," begged the voice of Miss Nomer. "It's urgent. There's been an incident and I need to show you something." Teresa displayed an insistence in her voice that painted her as clearly upset. Damen invited her to come down to his office, and she agreed before hanging up.

Not long after, there was a knock on the office door. Pierce got up to let Miss Nomer in and offered her a seat. Once both were in their place at opposite sides of his desk, the woman began to speak before Damen could say a word. "I had another nightmare, Mister Pierce. But this time, it came true! Another girl, another ritual, only this time I saw them take her to the woods in my dream. I recognized the area and I went there." There were tears in her eyes and no lie in her voice.

"Go on," he told her in a quiet voice.

"I found her, Mister Pierce! There was a girl there in the woods. She had a hole over her heart and she wasn't breathing. It was the same girl I saw in my dream!"

Pierce sat upright, leaning forth against his desk. "Did you call the police?"

"I did, but not until after I ran," she affirmed, sniffling through her words.

As he nodded, Damen asked, "You said you had something to show me?"

"I do," Miss Nomer said as she lowered the bag from her shoulder and opened it to reach inside. From within, she pulled out an ornamental dagger. The blade shone like the stars and the handle was a brilliant white moonstone. Theresa rested the weapon on the edge of his desk before she turned her eyes to him.

Her voice went cold. "I found this on the ground next to her. It's the same knife I saw in all of my earlier nightmares."

The room suddenly seemed colder and a chill ran up Damen's spine as though someone had just walked over his grave. "Teresa," he exhaled, "you can't take things from the scene of a crime. This has to go to the police." His logic did a decent job of hiding his true feelings: in truth, Pierce was shaken to the core. Dreams becoming reality seemed too farfetched, but he just couldn't shake the feeling that something truly may have been going on.

"The police do nothing!" she cried out in frustration.

"You're the only one who's even tried to believe me or do anything, Mister Pierce. Please, I had to show you."

Pierce sighed and offered the frightened woman a nod. "Alright. I'll take it to them myself. I have a friend helping me look into this. Tell me where you found the girl and I'll go and have a look." He lifted to his feet to move around the old oak desk and offer her shoulder a comforting pat.

"Oh, thank you Mister Pierce!" she sighed in relief. "I don't know what I would do without your kindness."

§ § §

That evening I was at a crime scene in the forest after an anonymous call came in about a girl that was bumped off and found there. She was wearing a flowing, white cotton robe that was accented with the brick red stains of her own blood. Apparently, she had been murdered by a blade through the heart. I remember speaking with the coroner when Pierce arrived at the scene.

Making my way over to him, I reached to shake the man's hand. "What's going on?" he inquired with his eyes cast toward the girl.

"Dead girl." I turned to face the scene myself. "Seems like it might be what you were looking for, Pierce. The white robe and all."

Just then, another Tin Lizzie arrived and out stepped Detective Rowe. The man was a real bluenose. Everything was by the book to him, and he acted like a hard-boiled goon.

He and I never saw eye to eye, and he was the reason Pierce left the force and started his private investigative service. We all had problems from the beginning.

After he stepped out of his Model-T, Rowe wandered over and glanced to Pierce and me with his nose in the air. "What are you two doing here?" Then, looking to the girl, the man scoffed, "Oh great, another one."

With a glance to one another, Pierce and I turned to Rowe. "What do you mean by *another* one, Tom?"

Rowe shook his head. "Not that it's any of your concern, but this is the fifth girl in the last two months we found. Same type of robe and all." He spoke with a matter-of-fact expression.

"Why haven't I heard about this?" I demanded.

"Because it isn't your case, Baber," he replied in his uptight way. "Also because we're trying to keep it away from the press until we can get it all sorted out. Now excuse me." He turned to head over to speak with the investigators on scene.

"Well, that answers some of your questions," I told Damen, turning to face him. "But this is starting to become a nightmare all its own."

Pierce nodded to me with a sigh. "She came back, Nicky. She said she had another dream about this place and this girl. She came here and found the girl and the dagger that she was killed with. Everything from her dream came true."

I looked at him in disbelief, shaking my head. "Pierce, how do you know that Nomer isn't the one bumping off these dames? Think about it—the information, the dagger, the dreams." As I spoke, the pieces seem to start falling into place.

"I don't know, Nicky," he sighed. "I don't think she was lying. For some reason, I believe her."

I reached my hand to his shoulder, gripping firmly. "Pierce, listen to me. You always have a soft spot for a sob story. You have to use your head on this one!"

Damen reached to pat my shoulder in return. "One way or another, Nicky, I think it's time I have another talk with Miss Teresa Nomer," he told me with a despondent look in his eye.

§ § §

After we went our separate ways, Pierce went back to his office and sat at his desk, reaching for his phone to contact Teresa. No sooner did his hand touch the receiver the phone began to ring. That was about as eerie as they come, and it made Pierce jump like a dog in a thunderstorm. "Pierce?" he said with an uncertain tone, and the voice that replied came all the more unexpected.

"Mister Pierce, I've had another dream," Miss Nomer reported. "Something is going to happen tonight, I just know it!" Her voice was frightened and as desperate as she was on her first visit to his office, but she still didn't sound as if she were lying.

"Alright, Teresa, calm down," he told her. "Tell me about your dream."

Miss Nomer went on to describe what she had seen in her

nightmare: the location was in one of the old mills in the industrial area of the city. In the dream, there was another ritualistic ceremony taking place and another girl was killed. Damen asked her to describe what she had seen of the location in as much detail as she could remember, and then assured her that it would be alright. He noted that the area sounded like the old Harvey–Felt textile mill that had been left abandoned before the war. The area was one of the lesser well-kept sections of the city and was a haven for shady deals. Pierce told her to stay put and that he would go and investigate the area. If his instincts were right, she was telling the truth and he would be able to catch these people in the act and possibly save the lives of future victims. If not, he would catch Teresa in the act. One way or another, hopefully it would all be over that night.

Once off the phone with Teresa, Pierce dialed my number. He was already on his feet and preparing himself to leave. After taking up his piece and fastening it into its holster, Damen turned to begin sliding on his coat. "Come on partner, pick up the phone," he whispered to himself.

I had been standing near my desk at the precinct after returning from the scene in the woods. There weren't many people left in the building at this hour, so everything was pretty quiet. When the phone rang, I leaned over to grab it. "Detective Baber," I answered in a tired manner.

"Listen Nicky. Nomer had herself another dream about a murder in the old textile plant downtown. I'm going to go and take a peep." His voice was urgent and low.

"No, wait Pierce," I urged him. "Wait for me to come with you." I reached down to open my bottom desk drawer, revealing the twin ladies I had resting within: a pair of 1911 Colt .45s that I kept close. One nickel plated, and the other was the blackened sidearm that I carried at my hip in the war. "Sugar and Spice," I had fondly named them.

"There's no time for the runaround, Nicky! If this is real, it may already be too late. I have to go." He hung up with me and left as quickly as possible.

After slipping on my holsters and packing my heat, I grabbed my coat and hat from where I had tossed them onto the corner of my desk and turned for the door. I had barely taken two steps before almost walking right into Beth, who had been standing directly behind me.

"I been lookin' all over for ya' Nicky," she told me, looking up into my eyes.

"I've got to hit the road, Bethy. What do you need?"

"I looked into that stuff you wanted. But it's strange. I couldn't find no records at all about what you asked. So I asked around. Ain't no one in the whole precinct ever had no talks with no dame about nightmares."

I frowned to her, shaking my head. "Well what about..."

She cut me off. "The girl? I called my friend at city records. There ain't no record of anyone named Nomer ever even been in Detroit," she said in a concerned manner. "Nicky, what's going on?"

The news dropped like a ton of bricks, and suddenly it hit me. It had all been a ruse. Miss Teresa Nomer wasn't real, and whoever this woman was she was spinning horse-feathers to Pierce. He had said that he was on his way to the mill that she had described, and he already could have been in danger. I grabbed Elizabeth and planted one on her.

"Thanks doll!" I made a break for the door.

§ § §

From the precinct, it took a good half an hour to make it to the old mill. When I arrived I found Pierce's car parked outside. My heart was in my throat and my hands were shaking like hypothermia. The man that once saved my life had walked into a potentially deadly situation, and I couldn't stop him. Hell, for all I knew Pierce was already dead. I hopped out of my car and drew Spice from her holster as I made my way for the front door. The area was dark from damaged street lamps that no one bothered to repair. The putrid stench of wasted life and the Detroit River filled the air. This, in and of itself, was something out of a bad dream. I had spent time on the front lines of combat burrowed in the trenches under gunfire, but even that didn't have my heart pumping like this. The damn thing was racing circles in my chest like a jackrabbit on dope.

As I approached the door, I noticed that it was already slightly opened. The frame was cracked as if someone had broken through. There was definitely someone inside. "Pierce?" I called hoarsely, swallowing against the dry frog in my throat. When I received no answer, I slowly pushed my way inside. "Detroit police!" I called. "If anyone is here, make yourself known!" There was still no reply, but I could hear sounds coming from the back. I glanced back toward my car thinking that I should have come with backup, but when I heard what came next I had little choice but to press on.

What sounded like a struggle came from the main floor of the mill back through the double doors just up ahead of me. I heard what sounded like a woman's voice, muffled and subdued, but she was definitely panicked. As I made for the doors, I suddenly began to hear chanting echoing within the room: low, breathy, and dark. I made my way up to the small crack between the doors to peek inside.

There were candles lining the floor in a circle around an old wooden table, and on it I could see a young woman in a white robe gagged and bound in place. She was struggling and frantic as another figure entered the room. He was dressed in a large, flowing crimson red robe lined with gold trim that was tied in front with a length of golden rope. Upon his face, the figure wore an old stone mask that was carved to look like the face of a frowning man with angry eyes and what looked like a crescent moon carved into the forehead. The chanting continued as the man rounded the woman, lifting a dagger with a shining white handle that gleamed brilliantly in the candlelight. He held the weapon with both hands, slowly raising it up over the girl's chest. I couldn't figure out where in the hell Pierce was. Maybe they'd gotten to him already. Though at the moment I couldn't worry about him; I had to make my move.

The doors suddenly burst open, splintering along the edges as the wood cracked from me kicking them apart. Raising my firearm, I took aim at the figure only to realize that the three of us were the only ones in the large, empty room that once housed rows of massive textile machines. "Detroit police!" I shouted. "Step away from the girl and drop your weapon!" The figure looked up toward me and I could see the dull, lifeless, blue eyes behind the mask. The chanting stopped suddenly, indicating that it was coming from him alone. There was silence for a moment, but only until the girl screamed through her gag. The robed figure stood there watching me before turning and walking slowly around the table toward me. "That's far enough!" I called, keeping my weapon trained on him; the threat of the heater pointed his way didn't seem to bother him at all.

Suddenly, the figure burst forth and ran straight for me. He lifted his blade over his head, closing the distance to sink his shiv into my heart instead of the girl's. I had little choice; I had to put him down. Two shots rang out, echoing through the large empty room like thunder from Mount Olympus. The figure dropped a few feet short of me, slumped over on its knees as his blood hit the floor. Well, at least I knew then that it was a human being and not some dark demon from a nightmare come alive.

The figure wasn't moving; he was just laying there. Kneeling down beside him, I reached out and carefully took hold of his shoulder and pushed him over onto his back. As he flopped over, the top of the robe opened leaving his chest exposed. I could see my two bullet holes where they tore into his flesh, placed just above a long scar that was on his left flank. It was a bayonet scar left over from the war. I knew this because that bayonet was meant for me, and Pierce had taken it for me. He had lost a kidney for me back then. I owed him my life.

My heart suddenly went from my throat down to the basement floor, sitting in my stomach like some bad bathtub gin. Slowly, I reached out and slid the mask from his face when suddenly my breath caught in my throat. All of my training, my years of service, and the things I'd seen abroad could not have prepared me for what was beneath it.

Pierce lay staring back up at me with a lifeless gaze. Strangely, there was an expression on his face that I could only have described as relief. With a shake of my head, I lifted a hand and traced it over his face to close my best friend's eyes and offer him his final peace.

Dropping back onto my caboose, I moved my hand up to knock aside my hat and run my fingers through my hair. "Oh, Pierce, what have you done?" I muttered to myself, but was interrupted by the sound of the girl struggling and screaming out in terror once more. Getting to my feet, I made my way over. My God, she looked exactly like Pierce had described Teresa Nomer. I removed her gag, and began to work on the ropes binding her to the table.

"A–are you really a cop?" she inquired nervously.

"Yes, my name's Detective Baber. What's yours?" I tried to remain as calm as I could so that I didn't spook her further.

"G–Gibbs. Annie Gibbs."

I nodded as I finished freeing her. "Annie, are you okay?" She jumped up and threw her arms around my neck, holding me in a vice-like grip.

"Oh please!" she cried, "Please help me! He had me locked away for weeks! I couldn't get away! He was going to k–kill me!" I held onto the girl as she cried for a few moments. My eyes were fixated on Damen across the room. What in the hell was going on? Was it him all along killing those girls? Why would he even have brought me in on this, and why the story of Teresa Nomer?

§ § §

It turned out that it indeed was Pierce behind it all. Apparently, the war had messed with his head in ways that no one had even realized. Now don't get me wrong here, Damen Pierce was once a good man. Straight as an arrow. He saved my life and did a lot of good for a lot of people as a cop and a private dick. Some things just stick with you that you can never erase. I never did figure out where the stories and acts of rituals and cults came from. The shrinks told me that it was just some delusional fantasy his mind created to give a face to the horrors he had left over in his head. Miss Teresa Nomer was a fictional person his mind invented. In his head, she looked like Annie Gibbs because the guilt he felt over his actions manifested itself in this way.

Hell, I don't understand all the mental baloney that the

doctors threw at me to explain it. The only thing that I can make of it all is that I think somewhere inside his twisted and confused mind, Pierce wanted to be stopped. Maybe that's why he came to me, the only person he had left that he felt he could trust and that he knew would look into the story and end his path of destruction.

It's been just about eight months since then. Annie Gibbs was questioned and returned to her family, safe and sound. As for me, I've since left the force and taken to my own. There were just too many questions and accusing eyes to sift through after having been involved in a case where my best friend was behind the caper. I had always planned to retire from the force one day and join up with Pierce in his private detective agency. He had always begged me to, but I just never gave in. So now it only seems right that I took over the business for him after his funeral.

It feels strange to no longer be with the department after so many years. It's quiet here, but this office somehow feels like home. At least it isn't lonely here. Wouldn't you know it, I'm not the only one to have left the force.

§§§

Nicholas stops typing and sits back in his chair, reaching to rub at his aching left hand. All that typing tends to cramp him up terribly. When the blood starts flowing to his fingers again, Nick takes up his glass and tosses back the remainder of his whiskey just as there is a knock at the office door. "Yes?" he calls out, turning to return his bottle and glass to the desk drawer. The door opens and his secretary steps inside.

"Nicky, there's a lady here to see ya'," Beth says, snapping her gum like a five-dollar pistol in a drive-by shooting.

"Show her in won't you, Doll?" He leaves his writing to be finished later.

"You got it, boss," she grins, heading back into the small room near the front door to the office where her desk sits. "You can go right on in, sweetie," he hears Beth say just before another woman enters the room. It seems that Detroit has no shortage of bombshells, that's for sure.

She walks in with a sway to her hips that puts most dancers to shame and is all manners of hypnotic. Lifting her hand, she adjusts the flowered hat that rests upon her raven black hair before she speaks. "I understand that you're a man who is good at finding people, Mister Baber." Her voice was everything feminine. "You see, my husband's gone missing and I found only this in his place." Extending her white lace gloved hand the woman rests a small curious object upon the desk. It looked like an animal made of paper that was folded many times. "Can you help me, Mister Baber?" she requests, watching him with eyes that sparkle like diamonds.

Nicky keeps his eyes on the strange, winged, paper animal on his desk. "Sure, I can help you." He sits back in the old, grumpy chair that groans its displeasure at every turn. This will be his first official case away from the police department. How difficult could it be? Nicholas would look into the missing husband… but that is a story for another time.

Time to

Wake Up

by Ashley Dearborn

She sat in Doctor Harts' office with a file folder clutched to her chest and an old, weathered shoebox resting on the floor beside her. She couldn't remember just how many times she'd been here, but this was the first time she had brought the box along with her.

The office was nothing if not clinical. Dull, white painted walls were adorned with a few paintings of flowers and plants that looked so generic they must have come with the office the way stock photos come with wallets. Behind the old oak desk hung several framed certificates displaying the many accolades of the Doctor's career. The furniture was upholstered with a soft, tan fabric that was covered with patterns of vines and faded red flowers. The fabric was likely designed to be soothing, but somehow seemed more unsettling than anything given the reason for this room.

Doctor Harts sat in the chair across from her with an expectant gaze. His eyes were soft and compassionate, in contrast to his stiff professional manner. "How did she die, Heather?" he asked her quietly.

It took her a moment to answer. Heather lifted a hand to wipe away a few tears before speaking through a sniffle. "They said she just stopped eating. They tried to make her, but... how do you force someone to live?" She shook her head. "She stopped responding to the medication, and just gave up." Taking a pause, Heather took a deep breath in an attempt to gather herself before she continued. "The last time I visited, she just sat in her chair laughing and laughing. I remember she looked so frail and thin, like a skull with skin stretched over it." The image sent a shiver up her spine.

Harts gestured to the shoebox on the floor beside her. "Is that it?" he questioned in his usual gentle tone.

Nodding slowly, Heather turned her tearful eyes to the box. She set the file in her hands aside and reached to pick up the box and open it slowly to reveal the carved wooden mask within. It was a deep brown in color, and the face was twisted into some kind of smirk; perhaps it was a grimace of discomfort. There were slits where the eyes would be and metal studs were arranged along the brow and cheek lines. "This is the mask she wore when she would... when she..." her voice was shaken as she tried to say the words, but instead could only break down again into a sobbing mess.

Doctor Harts stood from his chair and stepped to his desk to grab a tissue to hand to her before placing a comforting hand to her shoulder. "It's alright, Heather," he assured her. "It's never easy to lose a parent, even if they were abusive. It's perfectly normal to grieve for her and harbor hatred for her at the same time."

Still sobbing, Heather only nodded to him to show that she understood. It took a few minutes for her to finally control her emotions enough to speak again. "What should I do with it?" she wondered in a ragged tone. "I don't want to keep it around, but it's the only thing I have left of her."

The doctor looked to the fallen mask with a frown. "Hold onto it for a while," he instructed. "Just put it away somewhere. I'll have you bring it in for future sessions to discuss it further. For now, however, I'm afraid our time has ended. I have another appointment in a few minutes." He made his way back over to his desk and took up his pen, scribbling on a small pad that sat near his phone. "I'm going to prescribe you something to help you rest and settle your nerves a bit. Take this downstairs to the pharmacy and make sure you take them as directed."

Heather nodded and took the prescription as he handed it to her. "Thank you, Doctor Harts," she said in a flat voice as she lifted to her feet, taking up her file and hesitantly picking up the mask to put back into the box. Tucking both under her arm, Heather turned to head out of his office into the hall to take an elevator downstairs.

The trip to the pharmacy was always something she

dreaded. It always took hours to settle her mind after talking about the events of her childhood, but those first few minutes after the appointment were always the worst. Inside the elevator, Heather found herself once again thinking back to the events of those days. Remembering the way her mother would scream at her while wearing that damn mask, and lock her in the dark hallway closet. How she would talk to her through the door with her voice raspy and deep, as if it were the mask itself speaking. Or when she would stare down at her and tell her what a bad daughter she was, and how she ruined her mother's life.

Then there were the nightmares. Dreams of standing over a massive pit of graves that stretched out as far as the eye could see. Heather always saw herself falling into the pit before her mother would rise from one of the graves with a hazy green light emanating from her skin. She would screech about how bad Heather had been while tearing her apart.

Reaching a hand to wipe at her eyes, Heather drew a deep breath as the elevator doors opened with a cheerful chime that always annoyed her. The pharmacy sat directly across from the elevators. Next to it was a small waiting room in case you had to wait for a prescription to be filled or for an appointment. The place seemed empty aside from one lady working behind the counter. Heather stepped over and handed the paper that the doctor had given her to the pharmacist, muttering some small greeting while avoiding eye contact as she normally did when dealing with strangers. What conversations could anyone in this building really have anyway? It was a place for crazies, like her.

Accepting the script, the pharmacist looked it over with a nod. "You must have had a pretty bad day to need these, huh?" she commented in a tone that was all too lively.

Heather looked up sharply at the sound of the voice, ready to comment about how unprofessional that had been, when she found herself staring into the familiar slotted eye-holes of that haunting mask. The box suddenly seemed lighter under her arm, but it wasn't on the front of her mind just then. She choked out a sharp exhale as she stumbled back.

The masked pharmacist continues to speak to her, though her voice was now rising in pitch and changing to that familiar, raspy shriek. "A b–a–a–ad day. Bad, bad, bad, BAD!" Lifting a hand, the woman pulled the mask from her face to reveal the hideous, hateful sneer of her mother's face. Cracked, dry lips spread over yellow tinted teeth as she carried on, "It's time to wake up now, Heather."

She sat up suddenly in her bed, gasping for air with sweat on her brow. It took a few moments to realize just where she was, but soon she was able to stop her head from spinning. God, she couldn't even remember how she had gotten home. Did she go to the pharmacy? It was hard to tell what was dream and what was real sometimes. Turning to rest her feet to the floor, Heather lowered her face to her hands as she broke down crying, more because of her own weakness and confusion that out of fear.

She always kept the modest apartment lit at night, since she almost always awoke suddenly from the nightmares. A small lamp on the nightstand beside her was glowing comfortingly, and out through the sliding door of her bedroom she could see the living room lamp still alight.

After a few moments, Heather lifted her head once again and glanced around to make sure everything was alright. It was then that she spotted the bottle of pills that she was given sitting on her dresser. With a sigh, she pushed to her feet and shuffled along the cold, hardwood floor to grab them along with a towel before heading into the bathroom. Perhaps a nice warm bath would help her get some sleep, since she didn't get more than an hour or two a night anymore.

Heather began to fill the tub before turning to look at her pretty, young face in the mirror. God, she looked so worn out. The lack of sleep was really beginning to take its toll. After grabbing the cup from the sink, she filled it with water to swallow down one of the large, green pills with a gag. Then she removed her robe to turn and sit in the steaming tub. With a sigh, Heather closed her eyes and tried to relax. The water felt nice, but she truly had her doubts about it helping her sleep. She wasn't in there long, though, before she found herself no longer alone.

The door to the bathroom slammed open, revealing her mother standing in the doorway glaring at her through the eye slits of that wooden mask. She stormed into the room and grabbed Heather by the hair, yanking her head back to pull it under water. Even from under the surface she could hear the woman shouting at her.

With a choking shout, Heather sat up quickly in the tub, finding herself completely alone once again. She reached to run her fingers over her hair as she caught her breath and composed herself before glancing to the clock. Apparently, she had passed out for a good 20 minutes. Sighing to herself, Heather lifted her fingers, which had gone wrinkly from the water, and drained the tub before getting up to dry off and put her robe back on. Then she wandered back into the bedroom.

As she sat on the bed, Heather turned to reach for her blanket when she noticed something red move past her bedroom door out of the corner of her eye. Her heart began to race as she moved to open the drawer on her nightstand to pull out the small .38 caliber handgun and box of ammunition that she kept there. Fumbling to open the ugly snub-nosed revolver, Heather looked to the living room once more, but saw nothing out of the ordinary. Perhaps her mind was playing tricks on her again.

Frowning, she scooted to the end of the bed, trying to take a closer look. She was just beginning to think she was losing her mind when suddenly, several similar red figures moved past the cracked open door. Heather wanted to scream, but found her breath choked in her throat. The only thought in her mind was to get that gun loaded, though as it struck her mind to do so, she realized that it didn't feel the same in her grip. Looking down at it, she found that she was actually holding onto the mask. It's twisted face grinning up at her with the metal studs shining softly in the lamplight. With a shriek, Heather threw the mask to the floor and lifted her head to find four red-robed figures standing shoulder to shoulder at the foot of her bed. The hoods obscured their heads, but she could see that each of them was wearing that same, terrible mask.

"What the hell do you want from me?!" she begged desperately, pushing herself back against the headboard of the bed.

One of the four lifted a thin, withered hand that she would recognize anywhere. As it reached to slowly pull away its mask, Heather could barely make out the features of her own face staring back at her within the confines of the hood. She wore a knowing, triumphant grin upon her face as she spoke in a gentle, caressing voice, "It's time to wake up now, Heather." The words rang through her mind like a song, slowly changing in pitch until they were in a different voice altogether.

"It's time to wake up now..." she hears the soothing voice of Doctor Harts mutter.

Fluttering her eyes open, Heather finds herself in a small, white room. There is little else to furnish it save for a small, steel-framed bed, a window that has bars over it, and a small porcelain sink with a mirror above it. She stirs, trying to sit up but finds herself bound to the bed by large leather straps across her chest, arms, and legs. *No, not again! God, please no more!*

Dropping her head back to the thin, white pillow, she hears Doctor Harts voice as he steps around the bed to look down at her. "It's time to wake up now, Jody," he tells her with a smile.

Shaking her head, she looks to him with a confused look. "Wh–what? My name's not Jody, Doctor Harts. You know me."

The doctor frowns, speaking through a sigh. "I thought we were well past this, Jody."

"My name is Heather!" she screams at him, straining against the straps defiantly.

Lifting his chart, Harts begins to write something down. "Jody, we've been over this many times. Heather died, remember? She was seven years old when you killed her."

Her eyes go wide in horror before she turns her head to look over to the mirror that sits over the sink. The reflection staring back at her is something straight from her nightmares. Jody's face is weathered and thin, like skin stretched over a skull, and her hair is a stringy, gray mess. Her flesh is pale, as if she hasn't been in the sun in years, and her body looks malnourished.

As she stares at herself in confused terror, she watches her own face smile back at her from the mirror. The black-toothed expression is filled with fury as it speaks to her in her own voice: "It's time to start screaming now, Jody."

Ghost Seer

by Mel Ngai

After the tremor passed, Nadine found herself stomach-first on the tiled floor. She made one quick scan around and saw no one, even though her sister had been right next to her just a moment ago along with the rest of the students who had gone on the field trip. Londonderry High School itself looked intact; nothing had fallen or crumbled around her in the past minute. As she scrambled to her feet, she noticed a thick fog had engulfed the lobby and the hallways ahead, darkening them even more than the nighttime sky outside. Somehow, she could still see.

"Tami?" she called. When silence greeted her, Nadine called to her sister again, but she received no response. She next tried the names of the few people who had attended the field trip—Tami's friends, their parents, the teachers—and still, she heard no one.

By then, she couldn't ignore the biting chill and stiffened

air hovering everywhere any longer. How was it so cold in June? She checked her watch but saw that it was blank. It had said eight forty-five when she'd checked earlier, before the tremor had hit but after the arrival of the last bus of the field trip. The bus had returned only fifteen minutes ago, far later than all the others due to an engine mishap, or so Tami had told her over the phone. Nadine had taken the whole ordeal in stride as all she needed to do was pick up her sister and drive them both home.

Which, of course, she couldn't do right then—not when everyone had disappeared. She would've thought she was in either a dream or a wonderland, except her senses were assuring her that what she was seeing and feeling was real. Nadine even pinched her own cheek to test just that. The tinge of pain she felt confirmed her conclusion.

So what's up with this? she thought. *I hope to goodness my imagination's just acting up...*

That was when she saw a boy walking towards her through the fog. She didn't recognize him, and she couldn't recall if he'd been amidst Tami's classmates. He looked about seventeen, Tami's age, and was dressed in simple clothes of plain color. His hair was either brown or black, which made his skin look all the more pale. Whoever he was, Nadine realized he might've been the only other witness to the tremor.

Only one way to be sure, she figured. "Hello? Excuse me, but... do you know what happened? There was an earthquake, the lights went out, and a whole crowd of people just vanished—"

She noticed then that the boy had stopped moving. He was close enough now for her to see his face, the feature that struck her most. She froze as he regarded her with eyes widened, eyebrows curled, and jaw stiffened. Not once did he blink.

The seconds that passed dragged on like minutes, and all the while, Nadine heard her heart rate elevating. Despite her entire body's embracing itself to sprint, she tried to talk to the boy in a calm, steady voice. "Is something wrong?"

"You can see me," he said, his expression unchanging. "How? That shouldn't be. I thought you'd be like the others…"

"What?"

The boy stepped back and whipped around; then, to her complete shock, he faded into the fog like dust brushed away by the wind. She rushed forward to see if she could catch up to him, but he was nowhere near the orange lockers or in any of the alcoves that led to the classrooms of Phase Four. Did he really just appear and disappear like a ghost?

Or is he an actual ghost? she wondered.

"Whoa, wait a second! Who are you?" Nadine called, though her instincts demanded that she run. "Where'd you go? Hey!"

Violent rattling suddenly clamored behind her. She turned around to see what it was—and spotted a locker door shaking as though a giant, feral animal were trying to break out. Her mind blanked—she couldn't think, couldn't understand, couldn't move—and when the door snapped off its hinges and hurtled towards her, she darted out of the way on instinct alone. The door clanged as it collided with the floor, and Nadine didn't stop watching until she was sure it wasn't going to move again.

She'd just confirmed that when she heard more of that horrendous, metal rattling thunder all around her. In the next second, several doors broke away from their locker foundations and made a beeline for her. She jumped and ran, taking the first right turn she spotted along the way. Metal continued to crash close behind her, and she could hear more of them being ripped away to chase her. She bolted down the hall and up the gray stairs, stumbling as she went.

Nadine kept herself from falling and stopped only when she ascended the last step. Her memories of the school's layout reminded her that she was heading towards Phase Two—and more lockers. Rather than run forward, she pressed her back up against the wall, leaving the stairs to her right, and heard the doors that had been on her tail crash against the steps. Afterwards, nothing moved.

Okay, she told herself, *now breathe in… and out. In… and out…*

Once she had done that, she swiveled her head around to check for any sign that another part of the school might spring to life, but everything remained still. Her thoughts began to clear as she became more and more aware of a faint murmuring ahead despite her blood's pumping in her ear. They were the only sounds she could hear then.

She yelped the second she heard the boy ask her, "What's with you?"

Nadine searched around, but she couldn't see him anywhere. Wherever he was, he was breathing hard…

"You're not dressed like a priest or a nun," he went on, "and you were with a group of regular people. I thought all of your kind were associated with the church, but you don't look it. Are you?"

"What are you talking about?" she cried.

"You're one of *them*, though, that's for certain."

"One of who, and what? I don't know what you're—"

"I'll tell you right now," he said, "there's someone I have to find, and I won't let you stop me."

"*Wait* a minute!"

The ringing of locker doors cut her off as they slammed into each other on their way up. The ones that had chased her earlier came rolling into her view, scraping against the steps and the wall as they went. Nadine sprang off the wall and made a mad dash towards the end of the hall. She was almost there when her footing slipped, sending her stomach-down onto the stiff carpet. In the same few seconds, she felt both the sting of pain from hitting the floor and the *whoosh* of the doors' soaring over her head; then, up ahead of her, they barreled into the double-doors, knocking them off their hinges. Each chunk of steel fell forward and landed with a loud, dull *bang*. Somewhere within that chorus of falling metal, Nadine heard his voice.

"Damn it," he murmured between deep breaths, "no time for this, not when I'm so close!"

Some of her panic finally gave way to anger as she began

to realize—and accept—that the school was haunted, that the boy was responsible, and that she was terrified. Shaking, she remained where she was but called out to him again. "If you brought everyone in here… then you know what's happened to them, don't you?"

"That's right. They're asleep, and they won't wake up as long as they stay in this place. It's not meant for living people."

Nadine felt herself blanch at the thought. "Wait… does that mean you and I are… dead?"

"I am. You aren't," he answered, confirming her earlier suspicion. "You're not the first living person who's been able to walk around in this space between life and death just fine; there've been others like you. But for me, I can do all kinds of things here. Don't know how, but I've learned. You saw it."

She looked up at the pile of orphaned locker doors in front of her as she started to piece together more of her situation. As far as she could tell, the ghost boy could likely do whatever he wanted in *this space*, as he'd called it, and the doors were just a small sample. He also seemed to know where she was without needing to see her. Despite all he'd done, his breathing was unsteady, like he'd just finished a workout routine… which meant there was only so much he could do at any one time. Once she saw the opportunity, Nadine picked herself up from the floor.

The boy must've noticed because the tone of his voice grew tense. "Don't try to stop me. If you do, I'll have to kill you."

"And what exactly do you think I can do?" she retorted. "I've never seen a ghost before you, and I don't know how to fight; I couldn't hurt you even if I wanted to. All I want to do is find my sister and go home. What's your name, anyway?" Her heartbeat pounded in her ears, ticking away the seconds.

And then he answered, "John, I think. I don't remember who was talking to me or when, or why. I don't even know how long I've been here. But that'll change. I think I've figured out how I can leave this place."

"Really? How?"

"It wouldn't matter to you." Judging from how he sounded, Nadine thought he might've been raising his hands to his head, frustrated. His silence afterwards, followed by a sigh that must've come through gritted teeth, only reinforced the image. "You really don't know what you are?"

"Other than 'not normal?' No…"

"And you're serious about wanting to go home and that's it?"

"Yes."

He let out another breath, so the next time he spoke, he sounded calmer. "Then I'll make it up to you. No more attacks. You're still alive, so you'll be able to get out of here easier than I can."

"That's… kind of sudden. Why the change?" she asked. Right away, she listened for other sounds besides her heartbeat and their voices, but nothing came.

"I thought you were trying to oust me from here," he replied at length, "but you sound like you mean what you say… and we want the same thing. I have what I need, so you don't have to stay here. All you have to do is find any door that leads outside and go through it. Simple as that. Once you walk out of the building, you should be back in the world of the living in no time."

Nadine navigated her way around the fallen doors and fast-walked down the hall, swallowing as she went. "It's really that easy?"

"Yeah. I've seen others like you run out of here, and I've watched living people for… a long time. I've watched them for as long as I've been trapped here. But that's enough. Leave, and I won't chase you down."

"What about the other people you brought into here? What'll happen to them? My sister was in that group, and I'm not leaving without her."

By then, Nadine had reached the spacious main lobby where those soft murmurs became more audible, echoing off the white walls and the two square pillars in the middle. The murmurs were coming from somewhere above her, but she wasn't sure how much closer she was to their source. The air's knife-sharp cold was worse here, causing Nadine to jump and cross her arms over herself after she'd taken a few steps in.

"Okay. Take her," he said. "You're Asian, so she's probably this other Asian girl…" He made a curt grunt, followed by an *ah* of recognition. "I'll leave your sister at the front door of the school. After that, both of you can go free."

A light flashed by the entrance. When Nadine looked

there after the light cleared, she saw a figure lying on the floor where there had been nothing but a table and the vacant attendance office before. Nadine didn't need another second to recognize the figure as Tami and rushed over immediately to check on her. She was breathing, but the skin on her arm felt icy.

"Tami! Come on, wake up…!" She turned her head upwards, but the ghost boy remained out of sight. "What did you do to her, John?"

"Nothing," he replied, his tone flat. "She passed out once she was pulled into here, just like everyone else except you. I think she'll be fine once she leaves, though."

"All right, but… what about the others?"

"Don't worry about them. Go."

John didn't sound so tired anymore, which meant Nadine didn't have much time left to think of how she'd escape with Tami in tow. They were close enough to the entrance, and given her sister's small frame, Nadine knew she could carry her out in a hurry easily if she had to… but she couldn't move right then. She kept remembering the faces of everyone who'd arrived on that last bus.

Each student had leapt out of the bus like a bird's taking flight. Each one, including Tami, had been sweat-drenched and beat-red from the heat and lack of an air conditioner. They'd leaned on each other, tired but smiling, happy to have made it together but eager to go home…

"Well?" said John. "You have your sister. You can go now."

"When the Speedy Gonzales bus finally sputters in, I'll tell you all about the engine screw-up. Great Senior trip, huh, Dini?" Tami had sounded so cheerful over the phone, bubbling with the laughter that had already gripped her classmates. They'd be graduating next week...

Finally, Nadine asked, "What about everyone else?"

After a pause, John replied, "They aren't *all* relatives of yours, are they?"

"No, but that's not the point. Why not let them go, too?"

To that, he said nothing.

Nadine looked once more at the doors and took a deep, deep breath. She let it out after holding it for a few seconds, then reached down to pick up her sister. Once Tami was more or less standing, Nadine put her up front and held her sister between her left arm and her body before she shimmied towards the entrance. She pushed on the closest door with her foot and used herself to keep it propped open, but she didn't take a full step outside.

"I don't know if you can hear me, Tami, but if you can, call for help when you wake up." Nadine put both of her hands under her sister's arms. "And if I don't make it out... you be good, okay? Dini's orders."

With that, she shoved Tami through the door—which then slammed shut with enough force to throw Nadine onto her ass. When she peeked outside, she saw nothing but darkness, as if someone had plastered black paper over every pane of glass on the doors. She was catching her breath when she heard John.

"What are you doing?" he asked. "Aren't you going to join her?"

"I'm not leaving yet."

"What…?"

"You drag a bunch of people into a place that's not meant for the living, and then you insist on keeping them here, even if it might kill them by the minute? *And* you don't say why you want to keep them? That's just… no." Nadine brought herself up to a kneeling position. "Whatever you're going to do to them won't be good, will it? So… I have to get them all out of here. I don't know how, but—"

John let out a scream that bellowed through the lobby, and he sounded close enough that Nadine thought he was next to her for a second. Cold wind scraped by her like a rake across grass.

"John! What do you think you're doing?" she cried.

"Don't try to find me," he said. "The way out's right in front of you. Get out of here and forget about all of this! You have one more chance: leave *now*, or die! Understand?"

The nearby table rose up; at the same time, the entrance doors began to flip open and shut in rapid succession, drowning out any other sound. One of the doors leading into Phase Five broke from its hinges and flew towards her. Nadine scrambled to her feet and moved back, dodging both the door and the table, the latter of which missed her by a nail's breadth before crashing into the side of the attendance office. When the table hit the floor, though, its metal legs snapped off and shot at her like arrows. She ran and threw herself behind the remaining door of Phase Five. The table legs punched into it, pushing her forward.

She caught herself enough to go into a sprint just as the door began to fall towards her. Its landing sent such a strong vibration through the floor, Nadine tripped but used her hands to steady herself and straighten up. The soft murmurs she'd heard earlier were much louder then; in fact, they even sounded like moans—and they were still coming from above her. Wherever they were, she was closing in on them.

The fallen door flew up into the air. The maroon-colored ones from the lockers joined it as they formed a barrier behind and in front of her. Nadine saw the stairs leading up to Phase Five's second floor and tore her way towards it. She ducked under one flying door, but the end of her long hair was caught between two of them. Gritting her teeth, she kicked off the newly formed metal wall, leaving behind several strands of hair.

She bolted up the stairs, following the sounds of the moans—which led her straight to the library. Through the interior windows she could see all those who'd gone on the field trip, and they were floating, unmoving, and surrounded by glowing mist. Near the bookcases and staring at her over his shoulder was a smoldering John, whose visage was emitting the mist's light.

"Don't come in here!" he cried, whipping around as he spoke.

He finished his turn by throwing a punch at the windows— and a second later, the glass shattered and created dozens of gleaming broken shards that were poised to strike their target like a vulture's claws. Nadine was only a few steps away from the library's entrance; all she had to do was rush through.

But the glass pieces converged on her right when she began to move. She didn't stop; she kept going and dove, sliding into the room and scraping her chin and arms. She kept her face down and her hands over her head until she didn't feel the glass shards raining down on her anymore. Silence settled in and she rose, enough to sit up, only to wince from all the cuts and scratches. Somehow, just two pieces of glass were stuck in her, one lodged in her upper arm and the second in her left leg. She first locked eyes with John before she went to remove the glass as carefully as she could. At the fringes of her vision, she could see the other shards hovering around her.

Then, suddenly, they dropped to the floor. John did too, and he landed on his knees. His shoulders rose and fell with each breath he took. Nadine finally withdrew the glass from her leg, muffling her cry of pain, and tossed it aside. Without any other choice, she covered the wound with her free hand and tried to ignore the pain in her arm. She kept her eyes on John, and both of them remained still.

"Why didn't you leave? I gave you a chance, and you ignored it. All for what?" John gestured towards the field-trip goers with a swipe of his hand. "So you could see *this*?"

Nadine turned to look at them, then to him. With her head positioned in a way to let her see the rest of Tami's group on one side and John on the other, she asked, "What are you doing to them?"

John averted his eyes, but he didn't move. "No point in hiding it now…"

Hold on, she thought, *is he afraid of me? No, that's not it; he could kill me right now if he wanted… so why doesn't he? It can't be just exhaustion…*

He never once turned to face her while he spoke, but that glow kept shimmering. "I noticed it when I first brought people here. I was looking for a way out, but I drew in a group instead. One of them told the others to escape, and they left. The one who stayed did so to exorcise me once he realized I was a ghost and what I could do. I panicked, and I killed him. His spirit moved through here and then… I guess it went to the next world. But his body remained. It dissolved fast, but before it disappeared for good, I could still sense some life coming from it… and I could touch it. I wondered if I could take it into myself. When I did, I felt more alive. It didn't stay with me forever, but it took a while to disappear. A long while."

"No way," Nadine whispered.

"The next time one of your kind came," he went on, "he was with a normal girl who fell asleep once she was in here. I wound up killing both of them during a scuffle. Just like with the first guy, their spirits left, and their bodies lingered for a few seconds. I took what life I could from them, and while I couldn't escape just yet, I might've come close. Then I thought, 'If I do this enough, I might be able to leave and—'"

"You murdered people just to find out if you could bring yourself back to life? That's what you're going to do with everyone here? You son of a bitch!"

"I didn't do it because I wanted to!" John protested. "As a ghost, I can't leave here. Those people I killed? I couldn't possess them, or any other person, or even an object. I couldn't leave this building even with the last pieces of life I took. But believe me, I tried. Nothing else was going to get me out of here. I had no other choice!"

Nadine tried to steady her voice before she spoke again; she didn't want to risk setting him off a third time. "What in the world is so important to you that you think killing people and stealing their bodies would be okay? So you could, what— 'find someone,' you said?"

"Yeah," he said, his tone somber. John eyed her, then vanished and reappeared next to the sleeping group. "I want to find him… the one who last spoke to me. He was trying to tell me something, but I never heard it. All I heard was, 'John.'"

Nadine focused her gaze on him again, but he didn't turn to face her. "I thought you said you didn't remember who'd spoken to you."

"And I don't. At least, not his name… but I remember his face. The details are still pretty clear. He's out there somewhere, and I have to track him down. Whoever he is, he's part of that life I used to have."

"You think he can lead you back there."

His silence told her enough.

Nadine thought of Tami then, wondering if her sister had awoken yet. What was she doing now? Was she wondering where everyone had gone and how she'd arrived at the front of the school? Nadine had no way of knowing anything of the sort—and that struck her as lightning would a tree. She and Tami were on two different sides of an unbreakable wall, and she wanted to go back to her sister enough to find a way to open a hole in it. She'd just need a tool with the right amount of power to do the deed…

He was right, in a way, she realized. *He and I want the same thing.*

"Do you know if… what you've done, will even work?" she asked him.

He remained quiet.

"What if everyone you've taken in tonight doesn't give you enough of that life force? How many people do you mean to kill to find your friend?"

John finally turned his head towards Tami's group, then to Nadine. "Those people will be the last ones. There are plenty of them, so they'll provide more than enough. After that, I'll be done. I just need to last long enough to find him."

"You really want to go through with this, don't you," said Nadine.

He glared at her from out of the side of his gaze. "How else am I supposed to go back to the living world and find him?"

"Is he even still alive? Do you think he'd want to see you like this if he were?"

"Shut up. I have to do this."

"John, listen. I know why you want to go back, but you've still killed people to make it possible. You haven't thought this through as well as you think you have."

The glass shards suddenly flew into the air and surrounded the field-trip goers. The one that Nadine had removed earlier hovered right in front of her face—and in the next second, John was there, too. She leaned back, but she couldn't widen the gap between herself, the glass, and the ghost. Despite this, she kept her eyes on him.

"Didn't you say you had no idea how long you've been here? Your friend could be dead by now... and so could your family, and anyone else you might've known. They could be waiting for you right now in the next world. Even if they aren't, *you* can wait for *them*, can't you? They'll find you somehow."

"You're lying. You couldn't know any of that!" he said. When his hand latched onto her throat, she could almost feel the presence of a hand, a hand whose fingers were trying to claw into her as much as his sleepless, raging eyes. The glow around him and the floating crowd intensified, and the groans from the latter crested into a chorus of wails.

Have to get through to him—

"But that's just it," she managed to spit out. "I *don't* know if I'm right. Neither of us will, either, until we go to the next world... and there, you won't have to kill anyone anymore."

"Shut up, shut up, *shut up*! Do you want to join them so badly?"

"He could be... waiting for you... in the next world!"

The ghost looked between her and the others once, then twice. The glass shards drew ever closer to their targets. Nadine tried to steer away from the shard in front of her, but it followed and pressed itself up against her forehead. With the hand around her neck having become more solid, John's hold clenched tight enough to keep her from saying more. Despite all of that, she didn't close her eyes; she watched as he continued to look back and forth between her and the crowd.

I'm sorry, Tami, she thought. *I'm so sorry. Looks like I won't be going home after all...*

All of a sudden, the glow around the field-trip goers intensified before fading, quieting their cries. John let go of her and leapt to his feet. Though the glass fell onto the floor again, the chairs nearby rose up and whirled around the library. As they did, John made shout after shout, thrashing his arms at the walls or the tables. More glass shattered, this time from the windows that peered into a black outdoors. The chairs collided into the floor, the walls, the shelves, and the computers; but they missed Nadine, the students, and the chaperones. In fact, they missed completely. By the time the storm settled, the library was in shambles, but all the people were either on the floor or on the tables without a scratch.

Nadine peered up after having lowered herself to the floor during the onslaught. She searched for John and almost missed him because she could see everything that was behind him through his translucent body. He had dropped to one knee by one of the windows, resting one hand on the wall and covering his face with the other. She watched his shoulders and upper back rise and fall in time with his harsh breathing.

"John…?" she said.

He didn't respond. Another light began to emit from his body, which grew brighter by the second. For a brief moment, she saw him glance up at her. He floated upwards and drifted away from her, but then the light enveloped everything. After a few moments, she heard him speak again.

"What's your name?" he asked her.

"Nadine," she replied. "Why?"

"You're the only one of your kind who's ever asked me the same."

Air burst outward and walloped her like hurricane winds, and darkness overtook the light.

"Dini? Dini… wake up, please…!"

Nadine recognized the voice and opened her eyes. She was greeted by Tami, whose face was wet and still burned from the Senior trip. The younger sister clamped her hand over her mouth, her hair's cascading from her shoulders like curtains over a stage.

"Tami…?" asked Nadine. She shot up straight when everything came back to her, but her sister kept her down. When she'd calmed herself, she asked, "Are you okay? And the others—what about them?"

"I'm fine. Everyone is, but I should be asking *you* that question," replied Tami. "Oh, my gosh, what happened to you…?"

At this, the elder sister peered at her arm and saw that the glass shard she'd left there had been removed, and that all of her wounds had been patched up. Blood still seeped through the bandage on her arm, though. She spotted a few paramedics tending to the others who'd been trapped with her. Nearby, a pair of police officers was investigating the damage that had been done to the library, wondering aloud to themselves how anything of the sort could've been possible. She last glanced at the clock, which said the time was quarter to midnight.

John, thought Nadine. Aloud, she asked her sister, "What happened?"

"I must've fallen asleep in the back lobby because when I woke up, I was outside the front of the school," Tami answered. "I couldn't find you or anyone else, and when I tried to go back inside, the doors wouldn't budge. None of them! I went to every entrance I could find, too. When I couldn't get in, I called for help. Even the police had trouble going in! But after a few minutes, the doors opened like normal… and when we came in, everything was a wreck. Seriously, we thought someone had attacked the school. Thank goodness we found all of you not long after we barged in… especially you. I think they want to take us all to the hospital to make sure we're as all right as we look."

"I see. You did a good job there, calling for help."

"Yeah, about that…" Tami let out a short chortle and looked away for a second. "I think I might've had a dream when I was asleep for… I don't know, a minute? Anyway, I thought I heard your ordering me to find help if I could. Weird, huh?"

"Funny… I had a weird dream, too." In her mind, Nadine added, *It was actually real, but… you wouldn't believe me.*

"What about?"

"Maybe later. I'm really, really tired right now."

"Okay. I'm going with you, just so you know."

"I know that. You had a story to tell me, didn't you?"

"Oh, yeah! About buses and engine troubles and no AC!"

Tami was cut off, though, when one of the paramedics came back to check on Nadine. Two more officers came into the library then, whereupon he reported to his teammates that he'd spotted no one suspicious within the building. Another pair arrived a few minutes later to say the same about the outside areas. The six then made arrangements to see everyone out safely once they called for a bigger transport to accommodate everyone. The paramedics later moved Nadine to a stretcher and touted her to the ambulance. Tami was just a few steps behind the whole way.

As she was being wheeled out, Nadine didn't have to move in order to gaze at the night sky. A thin layer of clouds hid the stars and blurred the image of the half moon. She had seen the sight a few times in her life, but somehow, while going from the school to the ambulance, she realized she hadn't truly *seen* it, or when she would see it again. She wondered, then, if she'd be able to see such a sight if and when she moved on to the next world, as John had…

By then, she was in the back of the ambulance with Tami sitting beside her. Nadine turned her head to look straight up at the steel ceiling and tried to picture the sky beyond. With the image of the moon in her mind, she said, "Good-bye, John."

"Hmm?" said Tami. "Dini... who's John?"

She heard that? Shoot. The elder sister pursed her lips together, trying to think of how to answer. At length, she went with, "Someone who'd lost his way, but I think I might've helped him find it again."

"Oh... wait. When did this happen?"

"I'll tell you later. Honest." Before Tami could try to protest, Nadine said, "You tell your story first."

The younger sister eyed her elder and crossed her arms over her chest, but in the end, she yielded. Nadine let herself sink into the sounds of Tami's voice, the bumps the ambulance hit, and the constant subtle rumble of the moving vehicle. And as she did, she imagined John's viewing the half moon behind the cloudy veil.

The Weaver

by Crystal Baugh

I t was the type of darkness where you could stretch your hand and almost feel the emptiness clinging to your skin. I blinked, wondering if maybe it would clear, but it stayed. As far back as I could remember this emptiness had been my world. I took a deep breath and then realized that something *was* different. I could feel the air in my lungs—a sharp, stinging sensation prickling through my chest and making me want to cough. Releasing the air, I watched it curl with mist before my lips, exalting in that singular triumph. It faded quickly and the nothing resumed, no matter how I tried to recapture that sensation.

After several frustrating moments I managed to roll myself onto my stomach. From there I was able to push myself up onto my feet. My short, wispy brown hair fell into my vision for a moment before I shooed it away with an annoyed gesture. Another sensation washed over me—a sharp, biting pain in the back of my head, and instinctively I moved my hand to try and brush whatever was biting me away. There was nothing. Dizziness and nausea flooded me, and somewhere I realized that I hadn't been bitten but hit. Hit hard. Truth be told, I wasn't certain exactly how I'd ended up here. I surmised that perhaps it had to do with that thundering headache in the back of my skull.

As I dropped my head in defeat, I noticed the fog for the first time (or had it been there before? I was uncertain). It curled and churned over my ankles, clinging to my socks with hunger. The longer I stared, the more certain I was that whatever this place was it was very strange. "Focus!" I snarled and then paused, uncertain of the sound of my own voice. It took a moment before I felt I could speak again. "Focus," I muttered more softly this time. "Where are you? Who are you? And more importantly... how do we get out of here?"

Answering these questions seemed a simple enough goal, and I decided to tackle the most obvious one first: my identity. I had a vague notion that I should have a wallet with identification on me somewhere, but as I patted myself down I felt no indication of such. My jeans had no bulges in their pockets and neither did the army jacket. "Of all the things for me to forget..." I mumbled sourly as I gave up on the search.

I was angry now, with me, with the world, with the emptiness, and in frustration I let out a loud yell, wishing there was something for me to drive my fist into. There was no response to my anger. Not a thing changed, and for all my impotent fury the fog seemed unconcerned. Kneeling down I examined the fog more closely, trying to figure out where it was coming from and, if anywhere, where it was going. If it was going to—or coming from—somewhere, that meant there had to be something out there other than me.

It took a long while for me to determine where, precisely, the fog was going since it moved so slowly, but I could swear that I saw it inching to my left. I got to my feet and started running in that direction. After what felt like miles, I slumped to the ground panting. Nothing had changed. With each step I took the fog splashed up around my ankles, but there was no sound of my boots hitting the ground. The only noise now was the gasp of my own labored breathing. I wanted to yell again but instead I felt my throat close, and tears made my vision swim.

Giving up already? Ah, and here I thought you might be a little more driven, a little more focused, a little more… of a challenge. The voice seemed to come out of nowhere and everywhere at once, and I was absolutely certain that it was not my own. It had a velvety, almost feminine sound to it, but the depth suggested that it was impossible for it to be female. I fought back my tears while looking around me, but the emptiness yet yawned in every possible direction.

"Who are you? Show yourself!" I demanded. My own voice sounding shakier and more childish than I probably would have liked. Instinctively, I looked for cover of some kind, my reflexes screaming to get down. Nothing presented itself.

Show myself? The voice sounded amused, though this

time it seemed like it was almost in my ear. In fact, I could almost feel breath tickling my skin. I jumped, moving my hand to try and strike the source. Nothing met my fingers. *Very well I shall humor you.* A breath later the fog at my feet began to stir, swirling and slithering upwards as though in a wind that I couldn't feel.

There was a second before the ground at my feet churned, and I dove to the side to avoid a baroque-looking mirror that slammed upwards from the dirt where I had been standing. Just as I found my footing I felt the same tremor follow me, and I scrambled ungracefully out of the way trying to avoid a collision. I wasn't fast enough that time and the edge of the mirror sliced into my calf, causing a hot burst of pain to wash up my leg. The last few mirrors finished the semi-circle and, graciously, did not come from where I had been laying.

I pressed my fingers to my calf, feeling the warm, wet, slick sensation of my own blood. The heat felt alien in this place but it was somehow reassuring in an odd way. *Faster! You must be faster! You are wounded already and it has yet to begin!* The voice giggled gleefully, and I fought back the instinct to snap a retort in its direction and simply bowed over to put pressure on my calf. Oh, it stung. I grit my teeth and took a breath through them as I tore the hem of my shirt and started wrapping it tightly over the injury. It wasn't exactly hospital-grade treatment, but field dressing never was. The fact that I knew that gave me pause.

You're wondering why you're able to remember how to make a bandage but remember nothing of who you are, aren't you. Who are

*your friends? Your family? What of your wife? What of your…
lover?* The last words dripped with honeyed venom. *Do you
even know your own name?* It was mocking me—I could almost
taste it.

"How the hell do you know any of that shit, huh?
Fucking tell me! How do you know I have a wife?" I yelled,
my voice hoarse with fear and outrage.

*I know more about you than you ever have, even when you
thought you knew who you were.*

"God damn you! I said to show yourself, you son of a
bitch!" I demanded, my fists clenching again and bloodied
fingers sliding across my palm. I felt my muscles coil and I
started to shake as the adrenaline rush brought on by fury
began to flood me.

"Look up." The voice sounded less ethereal and, in fact,
came from exactly the direction it had told me to look. I stared
upwards, squinting into the darkness. The mirrors seemed to
go up for far longer than they should, and as I surveyed my
world I realized that they had surrounded me. I was trapped.
Seated rather languidly atop one of the massive mirrors was a
creature. It had to be what was talking to me, I surmised,
since there was nothing else there. It looked masculine from
this distance, the image created by the broad shoulders and
the abnormally sharp features, but something about it made
the gender hard to pin down. As I watched I became certain it
was female, and then that certainty faded as it moved.

"I have granted your rather rude request," it said, its
voice accented through pointed teeth. Its position didn't

move, but I could feel its presence shift somehow and it appeared to loom over me, "But you really ought to be cautious what you wish for, shouldn't you. That's what got you *into* this mess."

"Who the hell are you? Where the hell am I? Did you bring me here?" I couldn't speak the questions fast enough, and despite the definite ominous feeling I was getting from the creature's presence there was a distinct relief that I wasn't as alone as I had initially feared.

"So many questions," the creature drawled, shaking its head and making a *tsk* sound with its tongue against those vicious teeth. I got the impression that it was scolding me and the waggle of its finger in my direction only reinforced that sense. "I am known by many names, all of them long forgotten. Also, despite my joy in your company, I did not bring you here. In fact, here is not actually a *here* at all. It's more of a *there*," the creature said, as though that explained anything. "However, to make your life simpler I shall simply call myself The Weaver."

My relief edged into cautiousness and I narrowed my eyes. "A weaver of what?" The esoteric hoodoo nonsense about "here" not being *here* made no sense to me at all. The thing that I was talking to rose to its feet and began to stalk around the circumference of the mirrored prison in which I stood.

"Dreams and nightmares, thoughts and desires, perceptions and lies… I am everything and I am nothing! This place is a playground and *I* hold all the fish." That made even less sense than before, and I began to grow frustrated again.

"This place is nothing, since it has not yet been made. It's empty because *you* have yet to fill it!" Rage stormed across its face in an imperial march. "Look at what you have wrought!" It struck one of the mirrors with its foot and the smoky, reflective surface of the glass faded into a thick, humid, sanguine glow.

I staggered backwards, landing square on my ass as I watched the mirror twist and distort until it settled on the image of a woman. She appeared to be lying peacefully across the immaculate sheets of an antique four-poster bed, her head cradled in the cup of her palm as though sleeping. Her long, red hair was wet and matted down against her scalp with something thick and viscous. Blood. "*Jessica!*" I screamed, a lifetime worth of flashes of her face, her laughter, the warmth of her smile, and the touch of her skin in that bed her parents had given us on our wedding day appearing before my eyes.

The view spun and changed, showing the other side of her now, revealing that her chest and stomach had been ripped apart, intestines spilled across the other side of the bed and dripping lazily onto the floor. The view turned my stomach and I nearly retched, but the horror of it kept me transfixed. "What did you do to her!" I heard myself screaming.

The creature's grin grew slightly. "Oh, you *do* remember her. I had been afraid you might have forgotten. Most of the time that's how it goes. But you don't remember what happened? Such a pity. I had nothing to do with it, I assure you. Do you understand yet?" It sprawled out lazily across the top of the mirror with a smirk on its face. I wanted to remove that smirk with a chainsaw.

I could feel rage boiling in my veins and I let loose a punch into the glass. It fractured the entire length of the mirror, though the damn thing didn't collapse. I could feel wet heat and pain across my knuckles, but at that point I was too angry to give a shit. "Understand *what*, exactly? That Jessica's dead? Is that what I'm supposed to *fucking* understand?" My throat was raw from all the yelling and my voice was growing hoarse.

That grin never wavered. "You're still so blind. Foolish, foolish, foolish!" The last three words were almost in a singsong manner and it fluidly leapt to another mirror, like a cat on a fencepost. Its fingertips caressed the glass in an almost sexual manner, causing it to glow as well. A young man rippled into view, lain out across a military bunk. The name "A. Delahn" was on a patch on the heavy military camouflage jacket he wore. The man sighed and lay back on the bunk. He looked concerned, turning his head to stare at the clock. It read 2:49 in blood-red digital print against the black display. "What about *him*?" the creature asked again.

I could hear the name in my head. "Adrian," I choked while gritting my teeth. "He got drafted last year on his eighteenth birthday. I've been waiting for him to come home... He's waiting for me." Guilt and affection churned in a thick, heavy ball in the pit of my stomach. I'd been trying to find a way to tell Jessica since Adrian got drafted that I couldn't pretend anymore. And now Adrian was home. And Jessica was dead. We'd never get to have that conversation.

"Your *lover*," the Weaver chuckled, clearly enjoying my pain in some sick, twisted manner. "Ah, humans. Just a moment ago you were sobbing about the death of your poor, poor wife. Do you still not remember? Perhaps you do... you stopped crying."

"What the fuck do you mean? Stop speaking in goddamn riddles and tell me what the fuck I'm supposed to be getting here!" I wanted to hit the mirror again but my sense of self-preservation prevented me from doing so. I was bruised enough. The creature didn't answer with words and simply gurgled in amusement, slithering over to another mirror which, at its contact, became awash with that now-familiar crimson glow.

A dense forest, thick with night and shadows, was split by a single, lonely path that wandered its way in and out of the trees. Moonlight fell in irregular and pale blotches against the ground, illuminating very little. The Weaver hung upside down from its knees at the top of the mirror, bowing itself backward to poke the surface. The picture zoomed in, following the path until it revealed the figure of a man with his skull bashed in. Blood spattered the pavement every-where around him.

I stared at my own body in horrified recognition. My hand moved to the back of my head, reflexively, as I remembered the crushing pain that I'd felt earlier. The Weaver's laughter curled around me like smoke. "Familiar, yes? Do you understand yet, foolish boy? Do you remember what you did? It felt wonderful, didn't it?" Its whip-like tail curled around the mirror in a possessive manner as it continued to dangle there.

Nathan. My name was Nathan Langil. I had just killed my wife. We'd been fighting again and... I felt my knees buckle and I sunk to the ground. Something hot and wet started running down the back of my neck and I raised my hand again to the back of my head. It came away sticky and covered in blood. "N–no!" Weakness started to flood through me, despite the terror. I stared at my own body in the mirror.

The Weaver dropped to my side and whispered in my ears, *"Across the moorlands of the Not, We chase the gruesome When; And hunt the Itness of the What. Through forests of the Then."* I didn't quite know what he was getting at. I felt frozen as I stared at the mirror, transfixed.

Two men walked up to the body, their flashlights slicing through the darkness. The first raised a radio to his mouth, "Found something... looks like we got a corpse here." He crouched and touched the side of my neck. "Yeah, he's definitely gone." I willed myself to move. I was still here! I'm still in there!

"That him? Mrs. Langil's husband? Serves the fucker right. Looks like he never even saw it coming."

"That'd be him. Apparently the wife's brother found her and chased him but he got into the woods before anyone could do anything."

The second detective shook his head, "I don't know what

happened to him. His record was clean as a whistle… Why the hell would a kid like this go bad?"

"Who knows?"

The view changed and I could see the outline of something standing nearby holding a tree branch that glistened wetly in the light of the moon that was shining through the branches. The figure moved, and I could tell that it was definitely The Weaver's presence. The back of my head was aching fiercely, but through the dizziness I could see the creature grinning. It seemed to almost blend in with the branches, like it was almost one of the trees that surrounded the… my body.

I watched it stalk up to one of the police officers and raise the branch, a fierce, gleeful grin on its face. Images of the man being a crooked cop and cheating on his wife filled the other mirrors. I didn't much care why the creature was killing people, even if it was some twisted morality; I just wanted to get the hell out of there.

I forced myself up, rushing over to the mirror and clawing at the glass with bloodied fingers. "I'm here! God dammit, I'm here!" They didn't hear me and my body didn't move. The image started to waver and fade, the mirrors disintegrating into mist one by one. I tried to scream, but nothing came out. The Weaver was gone, though its voice echoed back to me as I looked for it. *"Into the Inner Consciousness, We track the crafty Where; We spear the Ego tough, and beard, The Selfhood in his lair."*

Then the darkness returned.

Never Grow Up

by Elizabeth Harvey

He started seeing them when he was a boy: strange flickers at the corner of his eye, little shadows skittering across the ground in the wake of people passing by. He'd told his parents that people were being followed by little shadows and they had patted him on the head and told him he had "quite the imagination". As the years progressed, the boy grew up and became a man whose name was Thomas. Thomas, the boy, liked to make believe he was an adult. He had a job and an apartment in London, but when he wasn't pretending to be a man Thomas still saw those strange little shadows.

Thomas most often saw the shadows around people like himself, little boys and girls pretending to be adults. He knew children in adult skins when he saw them. They walked with a little more bounce, they smiled more readily, and they laughed louder. The *real* adults scuffled past with their heads down and their shoulders hunched against some invisible and icy wind. They never had the black shadows. Over the years, Thomas started calling them Dream Eaters because he secretly blamed them for people having to grow up and lose their dreams.

Unlike all of those other adults, Thomas lived however he wanted to. If he wanted to eat his dinner in his underwear while watching cartoons, he did it. He could eat T.V. dinners every day of the week if he wanted to, and he never had a bedtime. He also regularly battled pirates all around his living room furniture and had an eye patch and a special sword that he'd fashioned from a stick he'd found in the back yard. It was magical, of course, and the pirates always lost.

It was while Thomas was at work one afternoon, staring out his window in one of the tall buildings made of glass and steel (he'd gotten the job there because he liked the building's shape) that he started seeing the little black shadows closer than he ever had before. They were crouched under his desk and huddling in his own shadow. Fear struck him and he tried to tell himself what his parents had always told him. "I have quite the imagination," he murmured to himself as he turned back to his desk and started writing up the report that his bosses were expecting him to do that afternoon. He worked as an accountant because he liked numbers. He found them soothing because they didn't have sad eyes and tired smiles.

You see, Thomas pretended to be an adult while he was at work, having to remind himself of that often. "I must remember that I am all grown up today," he would tell himself when he stepped into the building wearing the close-cut black suit with the crisp linen shirt that he ironed carefully so that it held the creases very well. His coworkers thought he was a very snappy dresser, and when asked who purchased his clothes for him he responded proudly that he did his own shopping, *thank you very much*. Often people were confused at his response, looking at him strangely, but Thomas never seemed to notice.

The phone rang and he picked up, "Good afternoon, J&J accounting. This is Thomas Woodsworth speaking. How may I help you?" His tone was chipper and bright as he sipped his coffee after answering the line. There was no noise for a moment, though the sound of a child crying in the background suggested there was some sort of person on the line. "I'm sorry. I must not have heard you. How may I help you this wonderful afternoon sir or madam?"

There was silence for a moment, the child in the background starting to cry more loudly. No one seemed to be soothing it and that somehow bothered him down to the pit of his stomach. He heard a whisper that he couldn't quite understand and then the line went dead, leaving Thomas staring at the receiver as though it had tried to bite him. The whisper, in his imagination, had been his name. "That must have been a wrong number. Besides, I told them my name when I answered." Beneath his desk, the shadows shifted a little. They squirmed and wriggled over his nicely polished leather shoes, though he didn't feel them there. Their toothy little smiles broadened.

The day melted onward, from one hour to the next, and he found himself realizing that it was time to go home to his little flat only a few blocks away. He swooped up his jacket and got changed before he thundered down the stairs to the main floor. When he was being an adult he never took the elevator—he just wanted to press all the buttons and had on more than one occasion. The staff had to fish him out one day when the car had jammed and since then he'd decided that the elevator was trying to eat him.

Even though he was an adult, Thomas disliked driving. Cars were just fine to ride in, but driving frightened him. He had a bicycle that he rode to and from work and special shoes to grip onto the pedals. As he mounted the bike and adjusted the shoes, he started seeing those shadows again, feeling fear creep up his spine as they rolled and jumped and tumbled nearby. Trying to calm himself down, Thomas reminded himself of what an imagination he had; his parents had always told him how bright he was. Having an imagination always was a sign of being smart, of course.

Silently, the creatures grinned at one another when Thomas' back was turned. They crept after him, prowling after the bicycle as though stalking him. The evening sun did nothing to dispel those points of inky darkness, though no one seemed to notice their presence. No one ever did, except for people like Thomas. People with extraordinary minds see extraordinary things, after all. Thomas pedaled towards home and looked skyward, as rain began to fall. Fat drops splattered onto the pavement, and soon the road and sidewalk were soaked along with Thomas's clothes. He laughed as he rode through a mud puddle and then considered the cleaning bill. He avoided the next one.

Thomas eventually turned into his garage, leaning his bicycle up against the wall and chaining it to the railing of the stairs. He had lost several bicycles when he just used to leave them on the lawn (and his landlady had gotten angry with him) so now he had learned to chain the thing up. Mounting the stairs he took them two at a time, springing forward like a gazelle before he came up to the landing of the second floor where his apartment was. He opened the door and surveyed his messy living quarters; they were just as he liked them. No one could tell him to clean up now, so he was enjoying the fact that if he wanted to leave his socks on the floor he didn't have to put them away. He also didn't have to do the dishes since he ate T.V. dinners (with dinosaur chicken nuggets, of course) and ice cream straight from the carton (though he had run out yesterday).

As Thomas stared around the room, he realized that he couldn't remember the fantastic adventures he'd been on the day before. Every day he made certain to have at least one adventure, often with pirates, and wrote them down in a little book. This morning he had forgotten to because he had been in such a hurry to be a grown up for work that day. He had a very important paper to finish, after all, and his boss was depending on him. He had told himself that he would write it down later—after all, he would remember. It troubled him a little that he had forgotten his adventures and this evening he simply felt too tired to go on one, so he settled himself in front of the tellie and turned on the news instead.

Eventually getting to his feet, Thomas wandered into the bedroom and shut the door, taking off his adult clothes and slipping into his pajamas. Yesterday he had felt inclined to leap up on the bed and start jumping on it. Today he told himself he was just too tired for that, so he crawled beneath the covers and fell asleep.

The following day he worked late, finishing another project for his boss. He felt important and powerful, despite all that had occurred the day before. Thomas promised himself he'd write in his little book that night. His phone rang again and he answered it. "Good afternoon, J&J accounting. This is Thomas Woodsworth speaking. How may I help you?"

The sound of the child crying was louder now and he sighed. "Hello? May I help you?" There was no response except for the sound of halting breathing, and then the line went dead. How unusual. It must have been that wrong number from yesterday, though he was starting to convince himself it was a prank caller. After all, what idiot calls the same number twice and just stays on the line like that? It was after hours anyway and he shouldn't have answered the phone.

Saving the project on his computer, he turned it off and got to his feet, folded his suit jacket neatly over his arm, and headed into the break room. He kept his spare clothes in there since he didn't ride to work dressed in his good suits. With the London rain, it was impossible to keep bicycle clothes clean and he didn't want to have to stay the day in a dirty suit. He pulled his backpack out of the closet and took it with him into the bathroom, changing in one of the stalls.

Thomas emerged from the bathroom wearing loose jeans, a grey t-shirt and a black jacket with his backpack slung across his shoulders. His backpack was waterproof to prevent his nice suits from getting wet in the rain. Walking out into the hallway, he hit the elevator call button and leaned against the wall, watching the windows. The sky was overcast and it was spitting rain disdainfully down onto the streets.

The elevator's arrival was announced by the ding of the mechanism. He turned to step into the car, punching the button to take him to the bottom floor. He had once always taken the stairs, but today he'd decided that it was much easier to press the button. He reminded himself that all those action movies where the elevator cable snaps were just that and that the elevator decidedly was *not* trying to eat him. It wasn't sentient, after all. The elevator ride went uneventfully. Thomas stepped out onto the ground floor, waving to the receptionist as he headed outside and into the London rain.

As he tugged his bicycle from the rack he frowned, wiping the water from his face. For the first time he considered learning how to drive. It was just because he was sick of riding in the rain, he told himself. Little black shadows he didn't see swarmed over his feet, clinging to the bicycle's spokes, their gleaming teeth bared in rictus smiles. Wiping the seat off, though he knew it would do no good, Thomas straddled his bicycle. Wetness seeped into his groin and he grimaced, finding the material extremely uncomfortable when damp. It chafed. Yes, he definitely needed to learn how to drive.

When he got home, soaked and chilled, he propped his bicycle in the garage space that was his, closing the door behind him before he headed inside the small apartment building. It wasn't a bad apartment—Thomas made a good paycheck every week and knew how to manage it. He had always been good with numbers.

As he stepped inside, his phone rang. It was odd to him because he normally didn't have people calling him at home. He tended to live a rather solitary life outside of work. The receiver felt cold in his hand as he picked it up off the hook, putting it to his ear. "Hello?" He thought his voice sounded a little hollow. The crying child was almost unbearably loud as it kicked in, screaming in his ear.

"I don't wanna! Don't wanna!" it wailed, making Thomas jerk the receiver from his ear.

"Whoever this is stop calling me!" he demanded before he slammed the phone down. It started ringing again immediately and this time he didn't answer. Instead, he headed into his modest kitchen and started making himself dinner. He'd promised himself ice cream after dinner, but by the time he had his microwave meal sitting on the tray in his lap he no longer felt like going out. As he watched the news, it struck him to question how that prank caller had gotten his home phone and why.

Thomas stopped paying attention to the chicken nuggets about halfway through (their legitimacy as "chicken" was questionable anyway) and his French fries had long since gone cold. It just didn't appeal to him, so he set it aside and watched the newscaster discuss the stocks in the current market. With rapt attention, he watched the numbers flickering across the screen as though comprehending them for the first time. After a while his eyes slid shut and he settled more deeply into the thickly padded couch.

Exhaustion took him and Thomas began to dream. Spreadsheets rolled on through infinity and he was chasing down an errant decimal that seemed to be attempting to escape. All the while it was chanting "I don't wanna!" and stomping itself against the floor. Thomas responded that he didn't care whether it wanted to or not, it had to join the others and behave itself. No matter how many times he made the demand, however, it would not cooperate.

He woke in a cold sweat, shaking his head and muttering to himself, "Accounting is far more terrifying than pirates." That affirmation had him calming down as he tried to remember if he'd shut his computer down at work properly. That thought compelled him to set aside the miserable excuse for dinner and get to his feet. He had better check that; he had been working on a very important account when he'd left and he didn't want to leave that on the screen.

In the corners of the darkened room, a little boy sat, watching himself on the sofa. His eyes were red and puffy and his upturned, freckled nose was running. In one hand, he had a pirate sword fashioned out of an old stick and an eye patch was hiding one of the little amber eyes. "Don't wanna..." he murmured quietly, stuffing his fist into his mouth as he stormed over and reached up for Thomas' hand. "Can we get some ice cream? You promised."

For a moment, Thomas could have sworn that he felt something cold on his fingers and the sudden thought that he'd promised himself ice cream popped into his head. "I shouldn't keep eating that stuff," he reminded himself. "It's got too much fat."

The child sniffed, his little hand dropping to his side and he shuffled back over to the corner, plunking down. The shadows rubbed up against him like cats murmuring empty, soothing promises that it would be okay. He knew it wouldn't; the shadows lied. Stuffing his fist into his mouth he started to cry, feeling very alone and forgotten.

A brief moment of sorrow washed over Thomas and he felt like he'd just done something dreadfully wrong. After a few moments of consideration he thought that it must have been that damn microwave dinner he'd eaten. He'd known better. It must have been past due and that was why he was feeling that tightness in his stomach. He went into the kitchen and drank some cold water, which didn't seem to help him feel any better. He figured that it would go away after a while. Turning, he headed to the door, swiping his keys from the hook beside it, and headed to where his bicycle was parked.

The rain slicked his shirt and ran down his back, and he grumbled quietly at the chill as he made his way back to work. The building loomed over him, dark and empty with the onset of nightfall. The windows glared down at him like eyes in the dim light of the streetlamps, and he did his best to ignore the creepy and uneasy feeling he had in the pit of his stomach.

He'd come to the building after-hours before. It wasn't something unfamiliar to him; his bosses had given him keys to get inside in case something needed to be done—he was important, you know. The elevators were off this late at night so he took the stairs—dimly lit by a quarter of the lights that were on during the day—up to his floor and headed back into the office area where his cubicle sat.

The only light to see by was the dimly flickering "exit" sign over the door to the stairs and so he barked his shins on his wastebasket as he rounded his desk. Cursing, Thomas fumbled for the switch on his desk lamp. The moment his fingers found the switch, his telephone rang.

Thomas stared at the desk phone in disbelief. He looked at his watch and scowled. It was well past eleven. Indecision filled him for a long while and finally he picked up the receiver, "Hello?"

"You promised! And now you left me alone here with *them!*" The voice that had been shrieking in the background was now yelling directly into his ear. It was loud enough that he nearly dropped the phone in startlement.

"I'm sorry. I don't know who you *are!*"

"You *promised!* I'm scared…" The kid had to be really young, whoever he was.

"Where did you get this number from? Who gave it to you?"

"I just know it, okay? You *promised* and then you *didn't.*" The line went dead, and Thomas was left holding a receiver that was blaring a busy signal at him. He stared at it for a few moments and then hung up the phone, feeling a creepy, uncomfortable feeling sneaking up his spine. That feeling of guilt washed over him again and he scowled, once more trying to figure out where it was coming from.

The lamp's light did nothing to forestall them. The Dream Eaters poured in from every wall in the office, slinking through the inky darkness to pile around Thomas' feet. He didn't notice them, but they were there. They slunk up the legs of his pants, coating his skin like oil. They weighed nothing, so there was no way that their intended prey would ever notice unless he was quick. They had been after him for years, but he had evaded them clinging to the edifice of his childhood like a rock climber on Everest.

Thomas shook his head, turning towards the exit with the intentions of going home. He took a step forward and then realized he'd forgotten to turn off the desk lamp. Part of him screamed to leave it on, that the darkness would eat him, but a moment later there was a calm confidence he'd never felt before. No, the shadows would most assuredly not eat him. In fact, there was nothing in them to be afraid of. Why hadn't he realized it before?

His eyes swept over all the cubicles and he started to laugh quietly, shaking his head as he reached for the lamp. It turned off with a click and he strode towards the stairs, muttering quietly about how he hated climbing all those steps. He did it anyway, leaving the building locked up and secure before he headed home.

Once he reached his apartment he was thoroughly soaked and absolutely convinced that he needed a car. What had he been *thinking* all those years of riding a bicycle? It was silly. Thomas couldn't quite understand why he had, and when he thought about it he decided he'd been acting rather childish. Lugging the bicycle into the garage, he leaned it up against the wall and removed his helmet, hanging it on the handle-bars before he stomped up the stairs to his apartment.

When he had gotten up there, he noticed the place was a wreck. Papers were everywhere, his half-eaten dinner was still on the couch, muddy footprints were on the floor and dishes were all over the kitchen. It looked like someone had thrown a tantrum of some kind, and he stared, rather embarrassed with himself that he actually lived there. It took him a while to come to terms with that fact and when he did, he sighed disgustedly. However, he'd deal with that the next day and he settled down onto the couch, flipping on the tellie.

He fell asleep there, waking to the quiet hiss of static that suggested to him that the broadcast day had ended and that it must be very late. The pale light of the television filled the room and cast strange shadows against the carpet—strange enough that they made his skin crawl ever so slightly. They seemed to wiggle and squirm and where once, not so very long ago, he would have yelped and run into his room and hidden under the covers, he stayed to watch them. After a time, he realized they wavered not because they were monsters but because the light on the tellie wasn't even. "Oh," he told himself, "All these years I've been afraid of monsters and it was just how the television was working. I wonder why I didn't think of that sooner." He got up and stretched, heading into his bedroom to go to bed.

He did not dream of pirates. Instead, he dreamed of long pages of accounting numbers and tickets for the stocks that he was supposed to be watching. He woke in a cold sweat, not because a pirate had drawn their sword on him but because the accounting numbers were wrong and he had tried to fix them. They hadn't wanted to be fixed. Laying for a long time in a cold sweat, he considered the dream closely and shook his head. "Accounting is far scarier than pirates are" he murmured as he rolled over.

He did not dream again.

If you enjoyed the short stories in this collection,
please assist the authors by submitting a review at:
http://www.amazon.com/gp/customer-reviews/
write-a-review.html?asin=0984293000

For more information about Divertir Publishing,
please visit
http://www.divertirpublishing.com/